Yellow Roses

Yellow Roses

STORIES BY

Elizabeth Cullinan

FOREWORD BY

Angela Alaimo O'Donnell

AN IMPRINT OF FORDHAM UNIVERSITY PRESS

NEW YORK   2024

Fordham University Press has no responsibility for the persistence or accuracy of URLs for external or third-party Internet websites referred to in this publication and does not guarantee that any content on such websites is, or will remain, accurate or appropriate.

Fordham University Press also publishes its books in a variety of electronic formats. Some content that appears in print may not be available in electronic books.

Visit us online at www.fordhampress.com.

Library of Congress Cataloging-in-Publication Data available online at https://catalog.loc.gov.

Printed in the United States of America

26 25 24   5 4 3 2 1

First Fordham University Press edition, 2024

Contents

Introduction: In Praise of Resurrection

Bringing a book back into print is like a little resurrection. When a writer's books are no longer available to readers, she disappears not only from the current literary landscape but, often, from literary history as well. It is as if the writer had never lived, never left behind a significant body of work, never played a role in shaping and co-creating the literature of her era, and of our own, as well.

It is a thrill then, even if not a *bona fide* miracle, to witness the resurrection of Elizabeth Cullinan's *Yellow Roses*, one of four volumes of fiction by Cullinan, in this new reissue from Fordham University Press. Cullinan's two published novels, *House of Gold* (1970) and *A Change of Scene* (1982), and two collections of short stories, *The Time of Adam* (1971) in addition to *Yellow Roses* (1977), testify to her well-deserved reputation as a gifted storyteller. Contemporary readers and critics, among them the likes of Richard Elman and Joyce Carol Oates, and more recent scholars, including Charles Fanning and Patricia Coughlan, who have reviewed Cullinan's books over the decades since they were first published praise them for her "complete dedication to the ordinary, to sensation, event, process, detail" (Richard Elman, *New York Times*, January 8, 1970), her "near-faultless craftsmanship" (Oates, New York Times, February 7, 1971), her remarkable "authenticity to felt experience" (Fanning, *The Irish Voice in America*, 334), and her "spare, exact elegance in style" (Coughlan, "Elizabeth Cullinan: 'Through a Lace Curtain, Darkly,'<HS>" *The Irish Times*, January 4, 2017). To these critical observations I add my own admiration of Cullinan's penetrating vision, her deft and timeless assessments of the human condition, and her often heart-stopping, always incisive, and sometimes killer, prose.

Yellow Roses, the third of Cullinan's four published books, was greeted with the same enthusiasm her first volumes received. After two distinguished books of fiction, discerning readers knew what to expect, and she delivered on those expectations. The book was listed among a handful of Editor's Choice selections in the *New York Times* (May 8, 1977), ranking it with new volumes by John Gardner, Studs Terkel, and Gore Vidal, celebrated male writers readily recognized by the reading public of their time. Seeing her title appear amidst those selections, it is clear that Cullinan's *Yellow Roses* was bringing something different to the literary table, a relatively fresh point of view—for these are stories that powerfully evoke the writer's own milieu, that of young women living in the Manhattan of the 1960s and 1970s in the throes of the women's movement and the sexual revolution. And yet, for all of their rapt attention to their historical moment, they simultaneously speak to us across time, fearlessly telling the coming-of-age stories of women making their way in a culture that neither recognizes nor rewards their talents and that is designed to curb their freedom. The conditions she writes of differ from those evident in our culture today in degree but not in kind. Cullinan is merciless in her evocation of figures that dominate women's lives: the condescending boss, the negligent lover, the patronizing doctor, the smothering mother, the feckless father. Her eye is fixed and unsparing. No one escapes without judgment, including the heroines themselves.

And yet, sharp-eyed and sharp-edged as they are, the tales Cullinan tells are tempered by the virtue of mercy. This is one of the many qualities I admire about Cullinan's work and her vision. Everyone and no one is to blame for the circumstances her characters find themselves in, reflecting the complexity of the flawed human person learning to come to terms with the broken world she finds herself living in. In addition, Cullinan's stories imply a generous theology, one which acknowledges the reality of what Irish Catholic Cullinan might term "sin" and the need for grace to help redeem our griefs and losses.

Irish-Catholic Identity

Cullinan's identity as an Irish Catholic is a foundational aspect of her history, her sensibility, and her artistic vision. Born in the Bronx on June 7, 1933, to Irish-American parents, Cullinan grew up amid New York City's Irish diaspora. She was educated at Catholic schools, the Academy of Mount St. Ursula and Marymount Manhattan College founded by the Religious of the Sacred Heart of Mary, where her imagination was shaped by a classic Catholic formation. Nuns in habits, jocular priests, statues of saints, rosaries, novenas, morning Mass, and meatless Fridays were the stuff of Cullinan's daily life. After her graduation from college Cullinan left her pious Bronx family behind to live and work in Manhattan. She landed a job at *The New Yorker*, where she worked from 1955–1959, first as a typist and then as secretary to editor William Maxwell, and eventually began submitting her own stories to the magazine. In Patricia Coughlan's words, "For Elizabeth at 22, beginning at *The New Yorker* in Manhattan was a startling transition: a short geographical distance but culturally worlds away" from the devout, conservative, Irish-Catholic enclave of her upbringing. Cullinan's job introduced her to a new world and served as an apprenticeship, of sorts, giving her the opportunity to type up—and pore over—stories written by the best contemporary fiction writers of her era, including Irish-born writers such as Maeve Brennan as well as American writers such as John Updike. "Working for William Maxwell was like nothing else in this world except reading his novels," Cullinan once wrote: "It made me a writer." Over the course of two decades, twenty-three of Cullinan's stories were published in *The New Yorker* and later would be collected in the two aforementioned volumes. At a relatively young age, she had found literary success.

The conservative Irish-American Catholic culture Cullinan emerged from dominates the novels and stories she wrote well after her liberation from it. The hothouse world of the pre–Vatican II Catholic Church provides the setting of her fine debut novel, *House of Gold,* and it haunts her stories as well, exerting its powerful influence in the lives of her characters. This is especially evident in *Yellow* Roses, wherein Cullinan chronicles the lives of a handful of heroines, young women raised in the Irish-Catholic ghetto who venture out beyond their schools, parishes, and neighborhoods only to find themselves living in a disenchanted world. As Cullinan's characters begin to move in a secular society governed by a saint-less calendar of days, they inevitably find their assumptions about life and the world view they have inherited to be out of sync with those of everyone around them. The challenges they face take a variety of forms, nearly all of them touching on the issue of embodiment and raising the question of what it means to be a woman in the modern—and still male-dominated—world.

Intersection of -isms

Cullinan's fiction depicts the clash of cultures she, along with many other women, experienced during her lifetime: the expectations imposed by Catholicism that women stay chaste until marriage, marry in the Church, bear multiple children, and spend their lives exclusively caring for their family *versus* the aspirations engendered by the Women's Movement encouraging women to pursue an education, devote themselves to a career, and enjoy the same sexual freedoms that men have long enjoyed, now made possible by the ready availability of birth control and, later, abortion. Cullinan's characters do not encounter these competing choices as abstractions but as felt realities that they—and we, her readers—are palpably immersed in.

One of the ways this felt reality is made almost corporeal for the reader is through Cullinan's careful attention to the body and the physical world it is located in. Her heroines are remarkably attuned to their flesh, the sensations it registers, and the ways it is scarred and wounded by the world. She depicts meticulously what it feels like to undergo surgery for ovarian cysts—to be shaven, given an enema, and to wake up from anesthesia: "Her insides felt soft and pulpy, as if they'd been taken out and picked over and then shoved back in, unsorted" ("The Sum and Substance"); to have a lover one no longer feels passion for: "Now she was like a diver exploring waters where her ship had gone down, examining the wrecked hull, recognizing how unseaworthy it had been" ("An Accident"); to receive sudden news as a seemingly stoic adult of the death of an innocent child: "Nora was starting to cry like a baby" ("The Perfect Crime"); to visit one's father in an insane asylum: "The doctor led the way around a corner that ended in a huge door. 'Here we are,' he said cheerfully and took out his keys and opened the door; behind it was a door made of steel" ("In the Summerhouse"); to feel the ecstasy of leaving Mass on a weekday evening and experience a visionary moment on the gritty streets of Manhattan: "By the time Mass was over yesterday, the sun had set, and as I stepped onto the sidewalk I had the feeling I was leaving one of the side chapels for the body of the church. The buildings were like huge, lighted altars" ("Life After Death").

It is this powerful sense of embodiment that teaches her cradle Catholic heroines the truth of who and what they are. After her surgery, at the end of "The Sum and Substance," heroine Ellen MacGuire comes to a realization that vies with the received Jansenistic notion that the spirit is more important than the body, a puritanical teaching prominent in nineteenth- and twentieth-century Irish Catholicism. Echoing scripture, she declares with new, hard-won certitude, "The body had the last word—and it had the first. In the beginning was the body. In the body the battle began. The body took the blows. Nothing was lost on it. Blows to flesh and bone, to the sense, the faculties—the body took them and felt them more deeply than mind or spirit possibly could . . . The body had its own insight, its own learning . . . The body might take its time but the body understood, the body remembered." Ellen is forced to come to terms with both the fragility and the wonder of her body and the mystery of being mortal. Previously she believed herself to be in possession of self-knowledge, but she suddenly understands this was never the case. Being embodied as a woman, vulnerable and yet empowered, has taught her this wisdom, and the formerly submissive, eager-to-please Ellen breaks out of the role defined for her by her Church and her tribe.

And yet, at the same time, Cullinan's fiction values the traditions that have been passed on to her and that she chafes against. Constance, the heroine in "Life After Death" who receives the visionary moment outside her church in Manhattan, states toward the conclusion of that story the reasons she loves the Mass: "During those twenty or so minutes, I feel my own past to be not quite coherent but capable of eventually proving to be that. And if my life, like every other, contains elements of the outrageous, that ceremony of death and transfiguration is a means of reckoning with the outrageous, as work and study are means of reckoning with time." What Constance—and Cullinan—recognize and celebrate here is the access to the transcendent that their received faith provides, the larger context of eternity within which to locate oneself and the meaning of one's life. Cullinan's stories constitute a simultaneous rejection and affirmation of an ancient faith tradition, a "both/and" rather than an "either/or," embracing a complexity that some might find puzzling, but that most readers will find compelling and true. These are the stories of real people for Elizabeth Cullinan. They are hers, and they are also ours. For who among us has not felt the friction of living with contradiction?

Given the excellence of Cullinan's work, its powerful appeal, and the recognition it received during her lifetime, it is unfortunate that her books fell out of print. She enjoyed the writing life here in the US and also in Ireland for a few years. She taught at the Iowa Writer's Workshop, at the University of Massachusetts, and, finally, at Fordham University in New York City for nearly two decades, the campus of which is located just a couple of miles from her former home in the Parkchester section of the Bronx, bringing her full circle. She retired in 1997 and continued to live in Manhattan until 2015, when she moved to Towson, Maryland, to be closer to her sister and nieces. Five years later, Elizabeth Cullinan died on January 26, 2020. The *New York Times* obituary (published

February 14, 2020) summarized Cullinan's successes and also gave some small hint of possible reasons why her work may have seemed less universal than that of her contemporaries. Cullinan dared to challenge the Irish-American male tradition, in the words of Patricia Coughlan, of writing about "ward bosses and henchmen, larger-than-life political fixers, tavern social life, and father-son relationships. With quiet irony but consistently, she resists assumptions that women's concerns and experience are supplementary to men's." Indeed, Cullinan's stories assume that women's lives matter just as much as men's—especially their intimate, private lives—an assumption that was likely not shared by a vast majority of readers, even in the 1970s and 1980s.

Happily, we are in a different place now, in part because of courageous women writers like Cullinan, and are able to recognize that her stories speak to us as truthfully and as compellingly today as they did when they were first written some sixty years ago. Thank you, dear reader, for greeting this resurrection, this rebirth, and this remembering of one of America's forgotten fiction writers with celebration. Feel free to spread the news broadly. As poet Anne Sexton, and close contemporary of Cullinan, once wrote, "The joy that isn't shared, they say, dies young."

Angela Alaimo O'Donnell
Fordham University

Yellow Roses

Estelle

My name has a calm, steady ring to it—Margaret—but from the start I was called Peggy, and a Peggy I strove to become, though in living up to my nickname I ended up being untrue to myself. Peggys are lively, gregarious, independent, a little unpredictable, whereas I'm naturally reserved and rather serious-minded.

I was named after my father's mother, and as a child I felt this to be both an asset and a liability. My father's family, the Fishers, were prosperous, but my mother's, the Norrises, had charm and good looks. Mother had seven brothers and only two sisters, whose names went to my older sisters, Alice and Ann. I didn't mind so much missing out on those names. Both my Norris aunts became nuns, and in the process their identities got dangerously confused, partly because for some reason Aunt Alice elected to become Sister Ann Marie, and Aunt Ann to become Sister Alice Ann. I say "for some reason" though I know my grandmother had a hand in the decisions, and my Grandmother Norris was high-handed.

My father has three sisters; his brother, my Uncle Bill,

died before I was born. My Fisher aunts are aggressive, worldly women—or they were in the days when we saw them regularly, but twenty-five years ago a quarrel to end all quarrels severed our relations with that side of the family. I was fifteen at the time and I didn't see my Grandmother Fisher till ten years later, when my sisters and I paid a visit to what proved to be her deathbed. She was eighty-three and had broken her hip and was living with my Aunt Molly, who served us small glasses of purple wine that tasted like plain grape juice and that said all there was to say about what Aunt Molly took it for granted the three of us had turned out to be, though grape juice was in no way indicative of her own style, which impressed me. She wore a long-sleeved black wool dress, used a cigarette holder, and addressed her mother affectionately as "Ma." Her living room was done in shades of gray.

My Grandmother Fisher didn't know what to make of the three lost granddaughters who suddenly turned up that evening. "Tom's girls," she kept saying, shaking her head. She was a mild woman who gave the impression, even at the end of her life, of being generally amused by things—by all things equally—and this bothered me when I was a child. As her namesake, I felt I should have been singled out, but she hadn't the restless turn of heart that needs to play favorites. At least that's how I see it now, though at the time I blamed my failure to attract her attention on the fact that I was the image of my mother, who was eternally at odds with the Fisher sisters. They had an Irish way of endlessly and pointlessly finding fault and they made my mother miserable. As the sixth in a family of ten, Mother hadn't had much chance to find herself, or even to begin to look. Instead, she simply took as her own the Norris family image of fun-loving extroversion, but in fact she's as reticent as I am and she was no match for her sharp-tongued sisters-in-law. All this seemed to stand in the way of my making a hit with my father's mother, and though I understood that it wasn't my fault, I minded. I was a Peggy and I expected to be preferred, but that's something I've managed only to a limited degree, and in the matter of supreme preference I've failed altogether. I've never been married.

My mother likes to talk of all the boyfriends I've had, and though she exaggerates, I've had my fair share. But I've never really come close to marrying any of the men I've loved. They've all been more or less the same type—wayward men, in need of a Peggy to make them toe the line, men who are thrown off when instead of making demands I accept whatever I get in the way of love. What I've generally got has been a kind of grudging attachment that somehow precludes, though it can also outlast, love itself. I lack the authority that I see other people call on in themselves as naturally as they call on their eyes for sight or their lungs for breath. I never cease to be amazed by the ease with which someone will single-mindedly lay claim to and possess someone else. I myself invariably see both sides of the situation, which is fatal in love, where to admit the other's doubts is to set that person free. The result is that I've never even been able to picture myself married except once, and the man in question was someone I didn't love. For that matter, Robert Patch didn't love me—we were in love with other people—but we'd been introduced in the hope that we'd hit it off and we did, famously but not passionately, though had the timing been better we might have ended up together, maybe even been happy. I remember thinking, This is what you do; you marry a Robert Patch and have a pleasant life and a house full of possessions. Robert was an art dealer, and we used to spend Saturdays at the Parke-Bernet Galleries. He had an acquisitive nature and my qualms with respect to ownership extend even to objects, but in other ways we were a lot alike, both of us much gentler than the characters we were involved with. We made what amounted to a study of ourselves, and once he gave me a kind of test, one of those psychological-game quizzes, of which I remember only the first question: "Who are you?"

Without hesitation, I said, "Margaret Fisher." Had I answered, say, "Tom Fisher's daughter," I'd have been revealed as overly dependent, just as the answer "I'm a lawyer" —or a doctor, or a teacher—would have indicated maturity, a sense of purpose, etc. By simply giving my name I avoided the issue, at least in Robert's eyes.

"Who's Margaret Fisher?" he asked.

"Margaret Fisher," I repeated.

He was nonplussed, and so was I. I hadn't realized that other people's names aren't necessarily as important to them as mine is to me.

At the parochial grammar school I went to, my mother was on the best of terms with the nuns, who considered her, on account of her two sisters, one of them. In fact, Mother herself almost became a nun. I think she must have wanted desperately not to enter the convent to have overcome the prejudice in favor of religious life that prevailed in her family, where it represented the one sure road to success. But Mother was much prettier than her two sisters. She also had a talent: she played the piano. Work as a music teacher opened up for her, and through her teaching she saw a little of the world, but the idea that she should be a nun—that it was the best thing to be—overshadowed her youth, and she seems never to have taken the young men she knew seriously, except for a fellow who, ironically, left her for the priesthood. It was shortly after this that my father appeared on the scene, even more ironically, for he was an exseminarian, which of course looked to my mother like destiny, and so she married him. But her glimpses of life on Central Park West and Riverside Drive had given her expectations that Tom Fisher was neither equal to nor interested in. My father is like his mother, mild and humorous, with no great ambitions in life, no lofty dreams. My parents made each other unhappy, and Mother often said she was sorry she hadn't joined the convent.

She was also sorry she hadn't named me after herself. That she didn't was because the name Estelle had come to her arbitrarily. She was the third daughter, and my grandmother's mother-in-law, a Julia, had decreed that this girl must also be a Julia. My grandmother refused, but her defiance stopped short of picking a name that belonged to some other relative, and so she named my mother after a suffragette she happened to read about one day in the newspaper. When it came to her own daughters, Mother was reluctant to commit any one of us to a name that brought with it no great family fortune of love, but as time went on, as her relations with the Fishers deteriorated and as I grew to look more and more like her, I constantly heard her say, "I was never so sorry about anything as I am that you weren't named after me." I had no such regrets. I worshipped my mother, but the name Estelle never appealed to me. It's too emphatic; it calls to mind the kind of face that stands out without being beautiful, a face with a sharp nose, or lips that are too thick or too thin. But even now that my mother is old her face is pretty and her expression is open and loving, and it makes me sad to think that her own mother was so indiscriminate in putting a name to that face.

My parents and my sisters and I lived on the outskirts of New York with Grandmother Norris, whose house was across the street from the parish church, St. John the Apostle. In its day, thirty or so years before I was born, the house had been comfortable enough and the street picturesquely rural, but in my day the house, the street, and the neighborhood were a step removed from squalor. And majestically arrayed on that crucial step was St. John's. My grandmother more than basked in the church's reflected glory, she traded on it. She was an admirable woman in many ways, but having raised a large family on very little money and very high ideals she felt entitled in her old age to put her own interests ahead of the interests of anyone else, even those she depended on, and this was her policy with respect to the house where we all lived—in dissatisfaction, sometimes in despair. She wanted to end her days there, which was understandable, and she wanted us to stay with her, which was unfair, but stay there we did, in the shadow of the church, which was supposed to compensate for the beauty and order that were missing from our lives. To an extent, I suppose it did. It was a magnificent Gothic building with twin steeples, bronze doors, and broad, immaculately kept lawns, and every Monday after school the children of St. John's were marched over there for perpetual-novena devotions. I looked forward to Mondays. My mother made the novena, too, and afterwards we usually went shopping—to the five-and-ten for thread, or buttons, or hooks and eyes; to the knitting store for yarn or instructions; to the butcher for a pound of round steak chopped; to the bakery for a cake. Sometimes these errands produced a coloring book or an ice-cream soda for me, but my mother's company was the real attraction. I usually had her to myself, and even if my sisters came along, my prerogative as youngest was recognized, and I clung to it; I clung to Mother.

Before we went anywhere after novena, she always had to discuss my sisters and me with our teachers, and the churchyard, which had swarmed with children, would be empty before Sister Hildegarde or Sister Veronica let her go. Sometimes those talks had repercussions. Out of a clear blue sky, Sister might say to me, "I hear you're quite a musician," when in fact I hated the piano and never practiced. Or if I wasn't raising my hand often enough in class I'd be asked, "Where's that chatterbox I've been told about?" With all my heart I wished my mother had kept my confidence, and the depth of my trust, though not my love, began to ebb as a result of her indiscretion. A barely perceptible but dangerous breach opened up between us. And into the breach walked Sister Ambrosine.

She was an affected nun who later taught high-school French, but she was principal of St. John's for six of the eight years I spent there. She liked to keep an eye on everything and to do this by surprising us, but on the afternoon I have in mind, or for that matter on any afternoon, we must have been glad enough to have her throw open the classroom door and stand before us. Sister Ambrosine was unpopular but she was better than geography or spelling or arithmetic. She swept into the room and over to the desk for a word with Sister Dorothy, the fourth-grade teacher; then Sister Dorothy stepped down and Sister Ambrosine stepped up onto the platform. "Will Peggy Fisher please stand?" she said. I did. Sister Ambrosine said, "I have an announcement to make." I was an obedient child and seldom got into real trouble, but much was expected of me, and my most innocent acts were sometimes construed by the nuns as unworthy of my connections. I stood there searching my soul, but there was no way I could have anticipated or protected myself against what Sister Ambrosine was up to. She said, "Peggy's mother has always been sorry she didn't name her little girl after herself, and so from now on Peggy Fisher is going to be called Estelle Fisher."

Had I been stood up and stripped of my clothes I believe the shock and panic would have been less. Naked I'd still have been myself—maybe all the more so—but without my name I was rendered null and void.

"What's Peggy's new name?" Sister Ambrosine asked the class.

"Estelle," they shouted back.

"Be seated, Estelle," Sister Ambrosine said. I marvel now at that child who quietly sat down in answer to the name that wasn't hers. "Good afternoon, class," Sister Ambrosine said. She stepped from the platform and swept out of the room again. Sister Dorothy once more took her place at the desk. The geography or the arithmetic was resumed, but from all sides I was taunted by the whispered "Estelle!" It followed me for days.

"Hello, Estelle!"

"Hello, Estelle Fisher!"

"Estelle, Estelle, go to hell!"

I refused to answer to the new name or to write it on my homework papers, and I didn't mention the incident at home, probably for fear of provoking something irrevocable, some measure that would be legal and binding. Neither did my mother bring up the subject. I realize now that Sister Ambrosine must have picked up a chance remark and taken it on herself to set things straight—and instead put a bend in my life that I've never succeeded in eliminating. As for Sister Dorothy, either she saw my side, or she didn't care, or she felt Sister Ambrosine had overstepped the mark— they might not have got along; feuds flourish in convents. In any case, she never made an issue of the change of name. As far as my classmates were concerned, the novelty soon wore off—probably they had second thoughts, too, about lining themselves up with Sister Ambrosine. Eventually, everyone reverted to Peggy, and Peggy I was for the rest of my time in school.

After I finished college, I worked for a while as a typist. We were rather high-class typists, the four other girls in the office and myself—all college graduates, all artistically in-clined, and, as typists, all amateurs. That was an office where good looks and nice manners were excellent credentials, and years of dealing with pretty girls and their typographical errors—years, too, I think, of private disappointment and bad luck—had taken their toll on old Miss Foster, the woman in charge of us. She was full of idiosyncrasies, and soon after she hired me she took exception to the name Peggy. "I think you should be called Margaret," she said. "It sounds much better."

At first my full name made me a little uncomfortable, but then it began to grow on me, even to ring truer than Peggy, and so I've more or less stuck to it. When I have to introduce myself now I usually say, "I'm Margaret Fisher," and, by the same token, with people I'm close to I tend to abandon nicknames after a while. Names are the primary images we receive of ourselves, and faulty though the images, inappropriate though the names may be, I take them seriously.

The Sum and Substance

When the doctor told her she had to be operated on, Ellen MacGuire was frightened at first and then, almost immediately, interested. Health is a state of grace, an unconscious state. Sickness comes as a revelation. "It's probably nothing," he said, "but we may as well take care of it right away, don't you think?"

Ellen said, "I guess so."

"Let's see, this is Thursday." He leaned across the desk, languidly turning the pages of an appointment calendar, his back to the wall where his licenses to practice medicine and gynecology were hanging. He'd graduated from New York University in 1959—probably, Ellen figured, when he was twenty-six or twenty-seven which made him forty now, but his face was heavily lined, his brown hair was faded, and he had a general air of exhaustion that made him seem elderly, especially when he spoke. "How about going in over the weekend and doing it on Monday?"

"This Monday?" She thought that was rushing it for something that was nothing.

"No use putting it off, is there, once we make up our minds?"

"I guess not," Ellen agreed but again she was surprised as he reached right for the phone, dialled a number and asked for the admitting office. She'd thought arrangements were made behind the scenes, but there was nothing more to it than to booking a room at a hotel.

"This is Doctor Ballantine," he said. "I want to bring a patient in on Sunday. That's the twenty-seventh." He put his hand over the mouthpiece. "Private or semi-private?" he asked Ellen.

"Private," she said quickly, picturing grim hospital rooms where two strangers were locked in mutual hostility and humiliation. She knew of this secondhand. She'd never been hospitalized herself, never been really sick except once as a very young child, but that sickness was critical though from all accounts she was the perfect little patient, so perfect that the pediatrician, who was childless, wanted to adopt her—or so the family story went. He was the second man on the case, brought in after the crisis which was the most vivid of her early memories—a sensation of the bed seeming not to be there, of trying to hang on with nothing to hang on to. Then her mother came in. "How's my girl?" she said, and Ellen let go, passed out. When she came to, the new doctor was there. He said it wasn't nephritis she had but nephrosis and he changed her diet. Instead of liquids there was chicken, eggs, bread, peas, lima beans—but no salt in anything, not even the butter.

"We're all set." The doctor hung up and then in a slightly too offhand voice he said, "Again, this is probably nothing but there's always the chance that when we get inside we might find something we don't expect."

Ellen nodded, as if he spoke for both of them, and in fact some such awareness, the suspicion that all is or could be not really well, lies at the heart of even our moments of the most profound composure, the sheerest bliss, but it lies dormant.

"However, I doubt that we have to worry. Lots of girls, especially you single girls, develop these ovarian cysts."

"Really?"

"Sure."

"That's some comfort, I suppose." She broke into a smile that was more than brave, more even than optimistic; it was positively merry, for something in his expression suddenly rang a bell. Once at the beach when she was twelve, a boy who was a little older had drawn obscene words in the sand for her, watching her reaction with just that same veiled look of importance. Confusion plus precocious skepticism made her laugh then, too, antagonizing the boy just as from the looks of it she'd antagonized the doctor. She said, "I'm a little nervous."

"Of course." He reached out and patted her hand.

"I've never been in the hospital before."

"Aha—a new victim."

Ellen guessed the joke was a standard from the mechanical way he offered it, as if he were recommending vitamins or asking for a specimen. What ever made such a flat man or, for that matter, any man become a gynecologist? Probably no great appreciation for women but not any aversion to them, either. Most likely it was the obstetrical side of the profession that appealed to him, the idea of a lifetime worthily spent bringing babies into the world. On his desk was a picture of his pretty wife and their three sons, sturdy little boys with spiky blond hair and faces that were all smiles— not, at first glance, much like their father.

"So we've got a date." With a spurt of energy, he pushed his chair back.

Ellen got up and said, "Thank you, Doctor."

"You can thank me when we're all finished."

"I'll thank you then, too." Her good manners were what

had won the pediatrician's heart though he was won under false pretenses, for it was sickness that forced the manners prematurely into bloom, sickness that absorbed her vitality and imagination, her child's giddiness and cunning, converting all that into what remained Ellen MacGuire's overriding objective in dealing with other people—not to be a bother.

"Till Monday, then." The doctor came out from behind his desk and walked her to the door, and they shook hands, and she left.

It was a beautiful mild April day. Outside the office, which was just off Fifth Avenue, a water main was being repaired and as Ellen went by one of the workmen looked up at her and whistled, and like a sleepwalker she came to. Something's the matter with me, she thought, maybe something awful. It seemed, more than anything else, unfair. I'm twenty-three, she thought. I'm nice-looking and I've certainly had good times but can I say I've ever known real happiness? She thought not. Sickness had very early given her the habit of looking beyond appearances. The discovery that she was not an ordinary, not a well child led to others even more serious—that her parents who'd seemed to be happy actually disliked each other, that money was scarce and that money talked, mainly late at night in angry voices, saying that there were limits to hope and obstacles to belief, that there might not really be enough love in the world to go around, maybe not enough to last anyone a lifetime. It amounted then to this difference between what things looked like and what they turned out to be, and as you grew older it became the real business of your life to try and make the two coincide, to be what you were endlessly advised to be—as if it were easy, as if you hadn't to find out first before you could be that: yourself.

She looked up Fifth Avenue and then at her watch. It was two forty-five. She was on her lunch hour from work, and half an hour overdue, but a bus was in sight, a block away.

The light was with her, and she set off across the Avenue, though without checking the side streets, and a taxi swung out from Seventy-fourth and almost clipped her, but she made the bus. Swinging on board, her heart racing, her blood pounding, she felt—she was struck by it—marvelous.

The hospital was run by nuns. In the lobby there was a huge crucifix, and here and there at the end of a corridor you came on a statue of Christ or the Blessed Virgin; there were pictures of various saints on the walls and a pair of oil paintings—one of the Archbishop who'd founded the hospital and one of the Pope. When Ellen checked in with her parents, visiting hours were just ending and the place was lively, almost festive, though the busyness and the noise couldn't entirely cover up what was the prevailing mood, a nagging recognition that change, not stability, is the rule in life. Ellen was reminded of graduation days at the convent schools she'd gone to. The same sort of uncertainty always colored those occasions and in her case with every reason. She'd never been a good student though she was intelligent enough. You could see that in her face, but the intelligence there was obscured thanks to a simple accident of nature, the mass of freckles she'd inherited from her father. They detracted from his looks, but Ellen had the benefit of what she'd got from her mother—green eyes, good teeth, a nice nose and very pretty, short, curly light brown hair. Still, the freckles were what first hit people in both her face and Mr. MacGuire's. They also stamped them unmistakably as father and daughter, and that Ellen might be her father's daughter as well was suggested by the way they stood together, a little apart from Mrs. MacGuire who was talking to the nun in charge of admissions. "I know, Sister, that religious are the very finest nurses," she said. "I feel I'm putting my daughter in good hands."

The hands going through the card file were quick and

capable. "Is that M-c or M-a-g?" the nun asked.

Ellen said, "M-a-c."

"M-a-c, capital G-u-i-r-e," Mrs. MacGuire said.

The nun picked up some loose cards and raised her eyes —the eloquent eyes, the steady gaze of someone who day after day looks mortality in the face without flinching, without flagging. "Here it is right in front of me—Ellen Mac-Guire, room four thirty-one."

The elevators were discharging crowds of the healthy and taking on hospital staff, for the most part, but there were also a few stragglers in bathrobes and slippers, leaning on canes or crutches, not so much victims as inhabitants of their fractures, their arthritis, their ulcers or diabetes, their pneumonia or pleurisy. It upset Ellen to think she belonged in their ranks and she was glad to escape at the fourth floor. The wide corridor was empty, and there was no one at the desk; then a nun came flying along, a young, thin, flustered nun of a type Ellen recognized from the convent schools— the type of nun who was never quite in control of the situation.

"I'm sorry to keep you waiting," she said, "but I'm here all by myself. We're always shorthanded on Sundays and we always seem to be so busy." A buzzer sounded. The nun looked at Ellen's card. "Around this corner, the last door on your right."

It was impossible not to glance into the rooms they passed and impossible to glance for more than a second at the gaunt figures lying in bed or propped up in chairs, flanked by flower arrangements that ridiculed the decrepitude of illness. "Four twenty-nine, four thirty—here we are," Mrs. Mac-Guire said, "four thirty-one."

It was a nice big room with pink walls. Ellen decided it would be comfortable. It was a new world. It would be interesting. She said, "Not bad."

Mr. MacGuire went and tried the armchair beside the

bed. "I wouldn't mind a week or two here myself," he said.

Mrs. MacGuire began taking off her gloves, finger by finger. This gave her time which she wanted, but time failed to give her what she wanted more, a way to make it seem as if there were nothing out of the ordinary. "Now don't worry about anything," she finally said.

"It's a minor operation," said Mr. MacGuire. "Why should she be worried?"

Ellen felt sorry for them. They were only bystanders at what was beginning to hold out to her unexpected compensations—the touch of morbid glamour, the suspense, the element of the unknown and the dangerous element of an adventure. She was anxious to set out on it and she had to hide her relief when the nun from the desk stuck her head in with a message.

"I'm afraid mother and dad can't stay. Visiting hours are over."

Ellen walked them back to the elevator. "Why don't you eat out?" she suggested.

"We're going straight home," Mrs. MacGuire said. "I want to be here first thing in the morning."

Ellen said, "If I were you I'd wait till they're through."

"I'll be here first thing in the morning. You be sure and have a good night's sleep."

Mr. MacGuire said, "In a nice room like that she'll sleep like a top."

The elevator came. "First thing in the morning," Mrs. MacGuire said. Ellen kissed her goodbye, kissed her father, waved to them and then went back to her room and over to the window. Four floors down was a short, typical Manhattan street. There were brownstone houses and budding plane trees and, at the corner, a drugstore and a delicatessen. The sky had been blue and clear all day and it still was. Though the sun was going down, there was considerable light—particularly vivid but ambiguous light that could as easily have belonged to a mid-morning in winter or an autumn afternoon as to this consummately springlike evening. Ellen stood drinking it in and then went and inspected the immaculate bathroom. It really was, she thought as she took the paper off the soap, a lot like a hotel. She might have been in a strange city, there to begin a new life. She looked in the mirror. The day before, she'd washed her hair. Her skin looked good, her color was high, her eyes were shining. She struck herself as someone ready for anything and she was smiling her readiness at the mirror when a timid voice called, "Dear, you're supposed to be in bed."

Ellen went back into the room. "I thought I'd wait a while, Sister."

The nun shook her small head. "You have to be in bed," she said. "For the tests."

"What tests?"

"The various tests."

At school these poor timid nuns were terribly taken advantage of. Girls talked out loud, walked around the classroom or out of it without asking permission, they lit cigarettes and sent notes through the air, and though Ellen was never an instigator of these tricks she'd never objected to them either, so it was in the spirit of belated remorse rather than strictly out of obedience to this particular nun that she unpacked and got undressed and into bed. She'd brought two books with her, two favorite collections of short stories. She picked them up, one in each hand, weighing their merits and her mood. Elizabeth Bowen or Ivan Turgenev— which? The Turgenev was the bigger book; she was going over the rich table of contents when there was a knock at the door and a young man came in. He was short and thin and good-looking with serious brown eyes and he was exactly Ellen's type. Walking into a party, she'd have spotted him right away and set about getting him to notice her, and it bothered her now to be the object of his amiable but strictly professional attention. "I'm your anesthesiologist," he said.

Ellen said, "I always thought it was anesthetist."

"Everybody does." He gave her a big smile. "But you're wrong, all of you." He put one foot on the bed, balancing a pad on his knee. "I have to find out all about you," he said.

Ellen would have liked to find out a few things about him. Was he married? Going with anyone? Was he from New York? It didn't sound so. He had a trace of an accent, not southern and yet stronger than anything out of the midwest; maybe it was a California voice. She wondered what had brought him to this small hospital and why he'd become an anesthesiologist. Did he like knocking people out cold? And what was he interested in besides medicine? Sports no doubt but, just in case, she moved her hand so that the name Turgenev was showing on the cover of her book.

"Have you any allergies?" he asked.

Ellen said, "Only hayfever."

"Any signs of asthma?"

"Are hayfever and asthma connected?"

"Sometimes one leads to the other."

"Not with me."

He made a note of it. "Have you ever shown a reaction to ether?"

"I was never operated on before."

"Good—a new victim!"

"I bet you say that to all your victims."

"As a matter of fact we do." He burst out laughing. As for Ellen, she was enjoying a joke on human nature. Because however deflating it might be to the loftiest view of that nature and however inopportune or unwise at a given moment, the fact was you could fall in love instantly and with practically anybody. Emotion was immediate and love, of all the emotions, the most so, but love was also the emotion most vulnerable to circumstances and right now these couldn't have been much less favorable. "What about illnesses?" he asked. "Is there anything interesting in your past?"

"I had nephrosis when I was little." It was something that always made an impression on doctors and, though she'd have preferred to make a different sort of impression now, Ellen wasn't sorry to have him whistle appreciatively.

"How little?"

"I was five."

"When the rest of us were getting measles and mumps and chicken pox."

"I had those, too—measles and chicken pox, anyway." After the nephrosis, it was an anticlimax. Ellen added, "I got the chicken pox when I was sixteen."

"I'll bet the other kids gave you a hard time."

"And I missed a big party."

He closed his notebook. "We'll try and see that you don't miss too much this time."

When she opened her book, after he left, none of the stories in the long table of contents appealed to her. She put it aside and picked up the Elizabeth Bowen and then had to put that down, too, as another young man came in. This was a heavyset fellow with black hair and bushy, black eyebrows. He looked as if something were on his mind and had been for a long time, possibly all his life. Ellen imagined a big family, not much money, a struggle through medical school and now the laborious routine of an intern's existence. She sympathized with him and wanted to put him at ease: "Gee, it's busy in here." He ignored the comment and avoided her eyes as he opened his little black case; inside it were needles, ampules, a length of rubber rope, cotton, band-aids. Ellen said, "My doctor just did a blood test last week."

"We have to do another, anyway." He tied the rope around her left arm and took her by the wrist. "Make a fist and keep closing it." She bit her lip and looked away. When she felt the needle, she let her fist slow down. "Keep clench-ing," he snapped.

"What's wrong?" she asked.

"Nothing's coming."

"Why not?" It was a stupid question but it seemed to her he should have answered it. Ignorance gave way to panic, and as he dashed around the bed Ellen wasn't perfectly sure she mightn't jump up and run off, or pass out, or disgrace herself in some unthinkable fashion, but what she did was what she was told.

"Make a fist." He knotted the rope on her right arm and stuck the needle in. "Okay."

When she looked, she saw the red tide rising in the syringe. It seemed to her she had plenty of blood, and if he'd had trouble tapping it then maybe that was his own fault. No matter what, it was wrong for him to act as if she were to blame and there wasn't even any need—she'd have blamed herself anyway. What did she know about her blood or her veins or for that matter any of her organs, even the nephritic kidneys. *Know thyself.* That had been the cry of a young man she was once in love with, and she'd taken it to heart. She'd studied herself and it seemed to her she had a pretty good idea of what she was, someone who was first of all honest—honest with herself, that is, though inclined to be secretive and even devious with others; not at all frank, really, ready and willing to say or do what a situation called for if that would make the situation easier. But she was reliable and cheerful and loyal and competent, submissive in love (to a point), quiet (to a fault) in anger, slow to take offense but, once she did, inclined to hold a grudge. She was also inclined to be jealous though she wasn't envious—she made the distinction there. Jealousy, she felt, had to do with what was yours and envy with what belonged to others, and it was her own life she wanted, not anyone else's. But she was passive with respect to what she wanted. Life had always seemed to provide for her without her taking more than the simplest steps, but when the need arose she could be decisive. There was no shillyshallying about her. And if she had little confidence with respect to how she struck others, she was, on the whole, at ease with herself though she did give a great deal of weight to people's approval—and this in spite of the fact that she herself was very critical but, of course, those two went together, just as shyness, which she sometimes suffered from, had to do with pride, which she also had her share of. And these things she knew about herself she'd have said were the sum and substance of her, but now there was no escaping the fact that they formed only part of the picture, for what did she know about herself physically? She was five feet four and had never weighed more than a hundred and six; she wore size five or seven, depending on cut; her feet were long, her breasts small, her waist narrow, and half the teeth in her head had fillings. She was susceptible to sore throats and swollen glands. She had good eyesight and a good ear. She tanned easily. She freckled. It was knowledge of a superficial sort, and she could see the need for improving on it. "From now on I'll remember which arm has the best veins," she said.

"You ought to." The young intern stuck a piece of cotton over the puncture, packed up his equipment and left.

Ellen took away the cotton. Beneath it was a neat, tiny hole; in the crook of her other arm there was a bruise where the blood had coagulated. She shivered and opened her book again, ready and willing now to settle down but unfortunately not quite able to. In her mind's eye she saw an anatomical chart, the inside of a body, all muscle and bone, veins and ducts and tubes, bathing and feeding the organs —coils of intestine, plump liver and kidneys and stomach, lungs, a pancreas, the famous heart, the precious brain. That was what the two young doctors looked at her and saw; whereas she'd looked at them and seen emotions, ideas, attitudes—all purely hypothetical. Yes, hers was a superficial approach. She admitted that, but she resented having to make an admission that so diminished the life of the mind. What was Elizabeth Bowen without her imagination and intellect, her wit and sensibility and passion and all the rest? Ellen went back to the book of stories and began sampling first lines till she hit on one that appealed to her: "The Carburys' two little girls, Penny and Claudia, went upstairs again with their governess, Miss Rice, as soon as lunch was over; their steps could be heard retreating along the pitch-pine gallery round the hall." Ellen lifted her eyes from the page to fix the picture in her mind and found that a woman had come noiselessly into the room. Ellen sat bolt upright. She was beginning to be a little annoyed by these surprises. "I'm certainly having lots of company," she said.

The woman was carrying a steel basin and a towel which she unfolded to reveal a razor. "Do you want to take that off?" she said.

"Take what off?" Even as she asked, Ellen understood. "My nightdress?" She definitely did not want to take it off.

"It's easier if you do."

Easier for what? Momentarily, it seemed to Ellen conceivable—but idiotic—that the razor was going to be used on her legs and her armpits. The reality was what seemed inconceivable—but logical. Stray hairs getting into an incision could probably cause infection. But how far down would this incision go? In her mind's eye she again saw the diagram of the human body—it was something to concentrate on as the razor grazed her belly and went between her legs. Bone, muscle, layers of tissue and membrane and, somewhere close to the skin, nerves that registered each sharp sting of the razor as it knicked her flesh and drew blood in half a dozen places, for the woman took no pains with her job but then why would she? It was a nasty job. It could only be done badly. When it was over, Ellen said,

"Thank you," and put her nightgown back on and picked up her book. Once again the two little girls, Penny and Claudia, went upstairs with their governess, but they and Miss Rice and the hall with the pitch-pine gallery had lost their appeal. Ellen laid the book aside and got out of bed, put on her robe and went to the window. It was getting dark. Lights were on in some of the brownstone houses, and the leaves of the plane trees shone under the street lamps. Across from the hospital, a couple were walking arm in arm. Suddenly they stopped. He gestured in the air and then slammed a fist into the palm of his other hand. The girl reached out to hit him, but he grabbed her by the arm. Ellen raised her eyes to the houses. Curtains were drawn across some of the windows; others were bare, and you could see an occasional figure cross a room. Like the pair across the street, these other men and women might be quarelling, they might be keeping hostile silence, or deceiving each other, but still the houses stood, the street kept to its course, the leaves of the trees didn't wither on their branches. Ellen leaned her head against the window frame. People's feelings —you believed they were the be-all and end-all but when you came right down to it how did they compare with buildings and trees? Not well. Feelings were treacherous. They drove you unmercifully and when you most counted on them they were liable to fail you, for desire could easily change to disgust, fascination to boredom; resentment, too, could vanish at a look and at another look anger turn to joy. Seen in this light, the quiet street with the stately houses was a misleading prospect, not to be taken as any index to the lives that were lived there and, this being so, it was depressing. When there was another knock at the door, Ellen turned away gladly and by now without any surprise at the intrusion. It was the timid nun with a tray of paper cups.

"I've got something for you to take before you go to bed. To make sure you sleep."

Ellen said, "I don't have trouble sleeping, Sister."

"Please take it anyway, dear."

Ellen said, "Oh." She was supposed to take the pill. As it turned out she was glad to have it. She'd lost all interest in reading and there was nothing else to do. At nine o'clock she got up and took the sleeping tablet and brushed her teeth and went to the bathroom. Looking at herself then, at the expressive folds of flesh where the woman had taken a razor to her, she had somewhat the same reaction, the amazement and the interest, that hit her when the doctor first said she was going to be operated on. It was clearer to her than ever that her understanding of her own nature was incomplete, and she had to wonder whether the rest of her thoughts and speculations—about other people, about the order of things in general—whether this might all be worth very little, all based on a fundamental misconception.

"Good morning, Freckles, I'm Hannie—short for Hanrahan."

Ellen opened her eyes and smiled, racking her brain for the thread of events.

"Short! Five foot nine and I'm talking about short!" The big nurse groaned. "Well, I suppose you feel like a nice breakfast—orange juice, bacon and eggs, toast, maybe some marmalade, a good cup of coffee. And what have we got for you instead?" She took an enema bag from behind her back. "Just the opposite."

Instantly Ellen remembered the night before—the strangeness, the unpleasantness—and, in the same instant, all that rolled back out of her mind. She laughed.

"Okay, turn over."

"You mean now?"

"Now or never."

Ellen made a face, but something told her this was hospital life as it should be—vulgar, yes, but wonderfully efficient.

There was an impression of things set unalterably in motion, and if these things were objectionable she had no cause to complain because it was all being done on her behalf. She could really only admire the way it was carried off—the enema, the alcohol sponge bath, the changing into a hospital gown, the first injection.

"This is just for a starter, Freckles." Miss Hanrahan deftly turned her over and stuck the needle in. "Wait till we give you the real stuff. Fly?"

If flying was what it was like, then it was supernatural flight, a state skin to beatitude. Ellen discovered in herself great stores of patience and generosity, tolerance and consideration. "This way?" she'd ask as they told her to turn or to lift an arm or leg. "Like this?" And when they apologized for sticking her with their needles or rolling her about she said, "That's all right. I don't mind. Go ahead.". She was grateful for everything that was done and she wanted to do something to help but she understood that all she could do was surrender to this course of events that seemed to have some purpose apart from her, a high purpose. The sight of her mother coming into the room brought her down to earth but she approached earth with new assurance and with magnanimity. She let herself be taken by the hand. She also let herself talk. "I've got a dress in the cleaner's," she said, "the green one with the pleated skirt. It's been ready for a week, so I guess it ought to be called for. And I forgot my hairbrush. Do you think you could bring one next time you come?" Mrs. MacGuire opened her handbag and took out a handkerchief. Ellen said, "Don't forget to call my office and tell Mr. Campbell how I am." Mrs. MacGuire's lips trembled. Ellen said, "Don't worry. There's nothing to worry about."

Mrs. MacGuire blew her nose. "How did you sleep?" she asked.

"Fine. They gave me a pill." An incomplete but chilling

recollection stirred in Ellen's mind, gave a dull warning, and sank again. "What time is it?" she asked.

"Nine-fifteen, Freckles. Time for visitors to clear out."

Ellen was feeling sociable. "Hannie, this is my mother," she said. "Mother, this is Miss Hanrahan."

"If she keeps talking, the sedative is going to wear off," the nurse said.

"I'll go outside," said Mrs. MacGuire. "I can see she's overwrought."

She. Ellen concerned herself from then on with this other, this she. She was the soul of good humor, laughing when she was given another injection, talking freely when anyone was around and when she was left alone, gazing contentedly at the light fixture on the ceiling as though it were a familiar and dear face. This face, however, she readily abandoned when the time came to leave. She watched every move the two nurses made as they transferred her to a cot and wheeled her out into the corridor. There she saw her mother and waved, not minding how public the gesture was because not Ellen MacGuire but she was waving and she was much more open and unselfconscious than Ellen, much freer and much, much friendlier. When the elevator came, she smiled around at the doctors and nurses already on board who had to make way. She smiled at Doctor Ballantine who joined the party at the sixth floor. Then, as she was wheeled into the operating room she burst out laughing. Theatre, it was sometimes called—imagine. It was tiled like a bathroom and it didn't seem very much bigger than a bathroom. Or was that on account of its being so crowded? She looked up at all the faces—unfamiliar nurses, the anesthesiologist grinning his grin, Doctor Ballantine and other doctors. They were standing there rather more aimlessly than it seemed to her they should be. She waited and, by the force of her own attentiveness, got everyone else's. What presence of mind she had, what pluck and what a wonderful disposition.

When they were all gazing down at her, she said, "It's not like this in the movies." Everybody laughed; then something was attached to her arm and abruptly, as if a switch had been thrown, she was out like a light.

When the switch was thrown again, there was a sense of existence having dwindled drastically, of having become an object, a slab of stone or a block of wood, something inorganic. Though it had no feeling itself, the object harbored a small, clever but terrified animal, crouched there, taking in a scene of frantic activity. Huge figures careened through indeterminate space, calling to one another. "Penny!" someone shouted, and the cry was picked up. "Penny! Penny!" came from every direction, the voices dragging long echoes, trails of exhaust that gradually made the space appear to cloud over and close in, revealing itself as a kind of ballroom stripped of all ornament except for a railing that circled it, very near the ceiling. Someone yelled, "Watch out!" The railing was loose. Anyone leaning against it would fall. "Penny!" they called. Penny was in danger. Footsteps pounded past. There was shouting—no, applause. Penny wasn't in danger, after all. She was at the movies. This was a theater, and Penny was sitting in the balcony watching the images slowly move across a tremendous screen, but the seats were no good. The figures were broken up—a torso, a shoulder, an elbow; then, suddenly a great menacing close-up: Huge eyes and lips, a giant nose, brown hair banked against a smooth white cliff. The big lips parted. "Have a look at this one." The frightened animal went for cover.

When Ellen opened her eyes, she recognized the ceiling light and was confident that it had been shining down on her for some time. With the same confidence she knew herself to be in the hospital, back in bed in her hospital room but consciousness, the pride of human nature, is arbitrary as to what information it will volunteer and what it will bury, and how she'd got where she was, where she'd been before this and what had happened, she had no idea beyond a vague awareness of horrors she had no desire to explore. She had no desires whatever, only an obligation of some sort.

"Take a deep breath. Go ahead." A nurse was standing by the bed. She had a kind face and a pretty voice. "Try."

Ellen felt her features twist and take on a look that she knew was ridiculous. It was a look of agony.

"That's it. Now try and cough. Go on. Try and cough."

Ellen was afraid. Her insides felt soft and pulpy, as if they'd been taken out and picked over and then shoved back in, unsorted.

"Go ahead. Cough."

Ellen pushed air down into her chest; her insides heaved and shifted dangerously.

"That's my girl."

She wasn't the nurse's girl, but was it the nurse who'd spoken? Ellen rolled her eyes in the ridiculous look of agony and found her mother standing on the other side of the bed, hands resting on a rail—the bed was railed. Like the bright light, this was a pressure preventing her from doing the thing she was expected to do.

"Take a deep breath," the nurse said.

"Try, Ellen. Please, dear."

There was a stand with a bottle hanging upside down next to her mother's face. Clear liquid was dripping from the bottle into a tube that Ellen discovered was attached to her arm. She moved the arm and was filled with a feeling of resentment. Something in general was unbearable and something in particular was a lot of trouble.

"Let me fix that." The nurse adjusted the stand and the bottle.

Ellen was horrified. The nurse could read her mind, and there were things in her mind that weren't meant to be known, but what things? It was vital that she remember and it was impossible.

"That's better, isn't it?" The nurse leaned across the bed. A pin with her name on it was fastened to the pocket of her uniform: *Miss Duross*. Ellen remembered a girl named Duross who was in college with her, a nice girl with long blond hair. What was her first name?

"Come on now," the nurse scolded. "Keep trying."

Jacqueline. Jacqueline Duross.

"That's the idea."

Ellen groaned.

"Now you've got it."

"Good, darling. Good girl."

"Now you're doing it."

They were wrong. Her mother was wrong and Miss Duross was wrong, but this came as a relief to Ellen, for if she wasn't doing whatever it was they wanted her to and yet they thought she was, then it was all right. There was no need to bother. It was doing itself.

She woke with dread in her bones and the taste of ether in her throat and the smell of it in her skin and her hair and in the bedclothes. She woke angrily, not having woken of her own accord.

"Would you like to brush your teeth?"

A short, gray-haired woman was standing beside the bed. From the corridor came a gash of electric light, but otherwise the room was dark. It could have been the middle of the night. Ellen said, "What time is it?"

"Half past five. In one hand, the woman held a basin; in the other were a glass of water, toothbrush and toothpaste; towel and face cloth were draped over her arm. She said, "Would you like to brush your teeth?"

"No, I wouldn't." Ellen was sorry to be rude, but she was miserable, miserable beyond anything she could have imagined and beyond anything she could hope to convey. She said, "I'm cold."

The nurse put the basin and the other things on the table at the foot of the bed. She cranked the bed till Ellen was half sitting and rolled the table up to Ellen's chest; then she went and closed the window. When she came back she picked up the toothpaste and said, "You'll feel better when you've washed your face and brushed your teeth. Shall I take the cap off?"

Ellen lifted a hand in protest and realized something was missing, something belonging to her—no, something attached to her. "The tube," she said.

"Here it is. Shall I take the cap off?"

"The tube in my arm."

"We relieved you of that. This is what you want."

Her fingers closed around the cold cylinder and immediately opened again. It was not what she wanted. "Here," she said.

"Certainly, I'll do it." The nurse unscrewed the cap, squeezed some toothpaste onto the brush, put it in Ellen's hand and then left. Ellen braced her elbow on the table and stuck the toothbrush into one cheek, then the other. The glass of water was towards the back of the table. It might have been across the room. She swallowed the toothpaste and let go of the brush. Her head sank to her chest.

"There now." The old nurse came back and wheeled the table away. "That feels better, doesn't it?"

Ellen said, "What was wrong with me?"

"Your doctor will talk to you about that."

When we get inside we might find something we don't expect.

"You can go back to sleep now."

It was still cold in the room. Ellen moved a leg in search of warmth and her insides seethed. She put her hand to the place; bands of adhesive tape held her together—barely, it seemed. She braced herself for trouble, but none came, and gradually her mind began to roll like a ball to the edge of sleep and back, to the edge and back, to the edge and not so far back, to the edge, balancing there: And then over.

Daylight woke her next, unequivocal morning sunshine streaming into the room and transforming it. Blue shadows lay on the bedcovers, like the bloom on clean snow. There were yellow flowers of sunlight on the bars of the metal bed, blinding sunlight in the eyes, flaming sunlight on the eyelids. Somewhere a telephone rang. There were people talking and dishes being stacked. Breakfast or lunch dishes? Was this a day in full swing or had it just begun? In either case, it was a day that belonged to invisible others who were able to make use of it. Ellen turned her face to the wall. Her hair was damp and wadded against her cheek. She tried to smooth it but her fingers curled like an infant's. She closed her eyes and let the tears come, infant tears of rage and confusion. Like an infant, she made no effort to control her tears and when she was discovered she cried, like an infant, all the harder. Miss Hanrahan hurried to the head of the bed. "What's wrong?" she asked.

"I don't feel well."

Miss Hanrahan stepped back. "Cheer up, Freckles," she said. "You'll dance again. You'll be back on the tennis court. Meanwhile, meet the gang." There were four of them standing at the foot of the bed, their uniforms immaculate, their faces made up, their hair done. "The two in basic white are your nurses, Mrs. Doty on the left, Mrs. Keegan on the right. The two in blue, Janice and Carol, are only students. Only—they'll get me for that."

The nurses had heard the joke too many times before even to pretend to rise to it now. The students had heard it just often enough to wish it might do some good and be reconciled to the fact that it wouldn't. As for Ellen, she refused to go along with this or any other joke. She said, "I'd like to know what they found when they operated."

"Leave that to the king of hearts."

"Who?"

"He's Doctor Ballantine to you, but to us he's Ballantine the Valentine."

"When will I see him?"

"He'll be around after breakfast."

"I don't want any breakfast." But breakfast was brought in just the same. "Please take it away," Ellen said.

Mrs. Doty set the tray on the high table and wheeled it up over the bed. Ellen remembered the early morning dark, the gray-haired nurse, the toothbrush. This nurse, too, would try and get her way but she'd get a fight. Things would be spilled and broken; there'd be screaming. Mrs. Doty said, "If you don't eat you're going to get gas and you don't want that, believe me." A warning and a wink—the nurse left it at that and went off. As Ellen lay watching the butter harden on the toast and steam rise from the coffee a desire took shape in her, not the desire to eat but to see if she could. She reached out with both hands and got the cup from the saucer, got it up to her chest, up to her chin —she could have taken a drink but instead she lowered the cup in disgust, leaving a trail of brown stains on the sheet. She felt very old, old and deformed. She had visions of derelicts crouched in doorways, of soldiers wounded and lying on the battlefield. It seemed to her that she shared their particular desperation, the terrible knowledge of how you could be engulfed by squalor, ruined beyond any thought of reparation by the wretchedness of your condition. The knowledge was more than she could contain, and this time her tears were the full flood that sweeps over people who've thought themselves past tears, people without bitterness and without hope. They came in spite of her and when she was discovered she tried to repudiate them, but it was the doctor who'd strolled in and he wouldn't accept her watery smile.

"Hey, what's this I see?" Whether it was the hour of the day, or the angle of the light, or a good sleep the night before, or a stroke of luck in his life, something, in any event, had drawn the lines of his face into an expression that was not exactly youthful but certainly energetic. "How're we doing? I know," he quickly answered himself. "Rotten."

The sympathy she'd felt the need of turned out to be an embarrassment. It showed her up. "I've been acting awful," she said.

"Go ahead and act awful. We made you feel awful. We took a lot of stuff out of you yesterday."

"What stuff?" she timidly asked.

"Nothing that belonged to you. Those cysts you had were pretty big though."

"But not—"

"Perfectly clean, just big and messy."

The good news was almost as shocking as bad would have been and almost as unwelcome—for if she was going to get better, was probably well on the way, then why did she feel as if she were going to die and why had she been acting that way? "Nothing's wrong with me then?"

"Not any more. We even gave you a bonus. We took out your appendix." He put up a hand. "No extra charge."

"Was something the matter with it?" Or had he wanted to make a routine job a little more worth his while?

"No, but you never know when an appendix will start acting up and you don't need it, anyway." He touched the the breakfast tray. "I guess you don't need this, either."

Ellen said "I told them I didn't want anything."

He wheeled it away. "They like to boss you around in this place, but you're not to let them. Tell them I said so."

It struck her funny—the idea of getting the better of the intransigent them. She started to laugh, but the laugh became a cough, and the cough turned to pain.

The doctor looked at his watch. "You're due for a shot in about fifteen minutes," he said. "Do you think you can hold out?"

"I don't know," she said hopefully.

"Moving around is what causes the trouble. If you lie still it should ease up." He patted her arm and left.

Pain—it was like a miraculous plant sprouting inside her stomach, sending down roots, putting out branches, flowering. She was obliged to accommodate this changing shape, conform to its erratic growth, contain the hideous bulbous fruit, the monkey-puzzle extensions that grew and grew. The plant reached its rare and ugly fullness and then began to die off. The flowers closed in on themselves, the fruit dropped, the roots dried up. Finally, where there'd been pain there was only the stiff shape of discomfort. Ellen thought she could get rid of that, too, if the bed were lowered. She jammed on the buzzer and didn't let go of it till she heard someone outside.

Mrs. MacGuire came in carrying three packages wrapped in silver paper, one stacked on top of the other, the topmost under her chin. Their silvery reflection plus the brilliant sunshine made her face, which was already shining with happiness, absolutely radiant. "We just met Doctor Ballantine in the hall," she said. The good news danced in her voice and in her eyes. Mr. MacGuire was the one who looked down in the mouth.

"Poor El," he said.

Ellen said, "I rang for the nurse."

"I know," said her mother. "I told her we'd see what you wanted."

"How do you feel, El?" Mr. MacGuire asked.

She felt as if she were going to die and there was nothing the matter with her. Ellen discarded the facts in favor of a half-truth that was likely to produce the least fuss and the most consideration. "I feel all right."

"And you are," Mrs. MacGuire said. "According to Doctor Ballantine you'll be as good as new, thank God." She held out her presents. "These are just a couple of things you might need while you're here."

Ellen said, "I wonder if you'd lower the bed a little." Mrs. MacGuire put the packages on the table and began to turn the crank; the head of the bed rose. "The other way," Ellen said, "the other—" A bubble of pain pushed up through her, lodging under her ribs—gas, just as Mrs. Doty had warned. "That's enough," she said.

"Poor El," said Mr. MacGuire. "Do you really feel all right?"

"Of course not really," Mrs. MacGuire said. "She'll be miserable for a long time and even when she gets back on her feet she'll have to watch herself very carefully."

She. Something between dream and memory came back to Ellen, the scarcely creditable image of a she who'd set off from this room the day before, laughing, making observations, being agreeable. But being agreeable wasn't what it was all about, not what it was about at all.

Mrs. MacGuire picked up her packages again. "Don't you want to see what you've got?"

Ellen said, "You open them for me."

As lovingly as she'd folded and tied them, perhaps only minutes before, Mrs. MacGuire now began to untie and unwrap the silver ribbon and paper, first from a jar of face cream. "Your skin gets dried out at a time like this," she said. "You have to take special care and give it enough moisture."

Mr. MacGuire said, "I think she looks beautiful."

"Certainly she looks beautiful but she wants to stay that way."

Ellen said, "I don't care how I look."

"You will, dear," said her mother.

The second package contained a big drum of talcum

powder. A trace of the scent penetrated the seal and clashed with the smell of ether. Ellen began taking shallow breaths that stopped short of the bubble underneath her ribs and well short of the warm, soft mess under the adhesive tape.

The last present was a bottle of cologne. "To cover up the hospital smell." Mrs. MacGuire began spraying some around.

"That's enough," Ellen said.

"Poor old El." Mr. MacGuire squeezed her hand. "Tell me how you really feel."

"I'm tired," Ellen said. "I'd like to rest."

"The best thing in the world," said her mother. "We had permission to see you first thing this morning but we'll go now. Later this afternoon I'll drop in again."

Ellen waved them away and began counting off: Time for them to walk down the corridor, time for a chat with the nurse at the desk, time for the elevator to be summoned and time for it to come and take them; then she bore down on the buzzer. It was still in her hand when Miss Hanrahan walked in flourishing a syringe. "This is what you want," she said, "right?"

Ellen said, "I want to go to sleep."

The nurse pulled back the covers and dug the needle into the thick, tough muscle tissue. "It's always lousy the first day," she said. "Tomorrow or the day after you'll pick up." She adjusted the bedclothes. "Do you want to lie flat?"

Ellen said, "Yes."

Miss Hanrahan wound the bed all the way down. "I guess I can count on you to ring if you want anything?"

Ellen took the question seriously. "I will." She lay for a while with her eyes closed, but as discomfort gave way to relief and relief to blessed comfort, she found that she wasn't really sleepy. Her mind was suddenly active. Pain, discomfort, relief, comfort—it was an enomous swing from the first stage to the last and each stage gave way to the next abruptly. Probably sooner than she expected, pain would start to push its way up through her again, but now there was this interval. It was like a homecoming, the happy repossession of herself; then, soberly taking stock. The worst was over. It had been terrible, but she'd got through it and now she was sorry she hadn't got through it better. She'd behaved very badly all around. She thought of the nurses—the anonymous old woman in the early hours of the morning, big cheerful Miss Hanrahan and the others, the girls with their hairdos and their makeup. She'd acted as if they were taking her life lightly when in fact they'd taken it on their shoulders. And the doctor—he must have thought she was an awful baby or an awful crank, but he hadn't shown it. He couldn't have been kinder. And it wouldn't have killed her to try and put up a front when her parents were there. It would have meant so much to them. They'd had enough misery to deal with over the years. Their lives hadn't been happy. They were both victims—victims of life and the way it punishes people who are weak as well as innocent, and victims of each other, of their love and need. And one night in bed, they'd created a different love, a different need, this Ellen, this she who was to make up for everything. But she failed them, too. Not that she wanted to, any more than she'd wanted, a few minutes before, to force them to stand by and share her pain. It hadn't helped. They'd understood it no better than she did. People went on about the mind and the body, and the body and the spirit, about which took precedence. That was all talking in circles. She touched her hand to her taped stomach. A knife had cut into her, sliced and probed and put things to rights. And now the cells were growing together the way the original cells had met and grown. She pressed on the tape. There was a burning sensation in the cut flesh; whatever they'd given her had worked only to a point, a point decided on by the body. The body had the last word—and it had the first. In the beginning was the body. In the body the battle began. The body took the blows. Nothing was lost on it. Blows to flesh and bone, to the senses, the faculties—the body took them and felt them more deeply than mind or spirit possibly could. Cuts, bruises, infection, disease, shock, sorrow—the body grasped them all at once and forever. The body had its own insight, its own learning. In its own way the body knew what happened and what to make of it. The body might take its time but the body understood, the body remembered.

In the
Summerhouse

The air-conditioning in the train was up too high. Mrs. Ganley got a headache the minute she stepped into the car, and her daughter Angela broke out in gooseflesh. Halfway down the aisle, they found a seat together, and Mrs. Ganley stepped back to let Angela slide in next to the window, as though Angela were a child and not a grown woman, twenty-six years old, but Angela didn't raise any objections, especially since there was no great advantage in sitting by this window. The glass had been hit—probably by a rock thrown on a dark evening by some poverty-stricken child at the lucky commuters passing over the city slums on their way to the beautiful suburbs this train was riding through now. The rock had left a mark like a bullet hole, with a sunburst of icy cracks that gave Angela the feeling that the freezing inside of the train and the ninety-degree weather outside were one and the same sensation. Like chills and fever, she thought, and rubbed her arms.

Mrs. Ganley said, "We should have brought sweaters."

"It's only a few minutes' ride." People said Angela was the picture of her mother as a young woman, and you could see the truth of that very clearly at the moment. Unhappiness can give faces a kind of intangible likeness, and unhappiness only had to bring out in their two faces what already belonged there—the real likeness that, year by year, their difference in age tended more and more to misrepresent. Unhappiness also seemed to suit their looks. Brown eyes, wide mouth, high forehead—features like these can gain from trouble, the way a dark mood will sometimes seem dramatic on a dark day. And Mrs. Ganley and Angela were both serious-minded to begin with, though Mrs. Ganley didn't know she was, and Angela did, which made her less so and her mother more. This was the basic difference between them. It was very basic.

Mrs. Ganley said, "It's always best to be on the safe side."

How hard, thought Angela, how little comfort it must be to produce a replica of yourself and have that replica turn out to be yourself plus something you couldn't make head nor tail of. "I won't catch cold," she said. "I never catch cold the ways you're supposed to."

"You're not supposed to catch cold at all."

Angela turned to the window. It was a perfect summer Sunday afternoon. The sky was cloudless, the air clear, the heat dry. The trees and hedges around the substantial Westchester County houses were as full and heavy and still as if they'd been painted, and the effect of the cracked window was to take the classical scene and make it modern, an abstract—the work, thought Angela, of a man who'd had his dream of happiness all of a sudden turn to unmitigated and perfectly coherent sorrow. Strange, how for some people life could be shattered and still hold its shape, and for others, when things went, they went completely to pieces.

"Mamaroneck Station next," the conductor called, and Angela's brain reeled off a little piece of nonsense her father had made up for her and her older sister when they were children:

> Sing a song of sixpence,
> A pocketful of rye,
> Four and twenty blackbirds
> Baked in a pie;
> When the pie was opened,
> The birds began to cry,
> "Larchmont, Mamaroneck,
> Harrison, and Rye!"

People had always said he was like a brother to them, as if that were some special dispensation they'd been granted, when what it proved to be was a deprivation. They'd missed out on whatever it was fathers were supposed to give or at least be able to give. What was that—protection? Some particular kind of concern? Some special attentiveness? The benefit of their experience, anyway. But it seemed to Angela that whatever had happened in her father's life left no benefits behind—not even for himself, much less anyone else. What about love?

Mrs. Ganley said, "I wish you'd worn your pink linen."

Angela had on a blue-and-white striped dress, something she wore to work when she had no place to go afterward. "This is more comfortable," she said.

"But you always look so well set up in your pink linen."

Love. If you could say that love was play, then you could say her father loved his daughters, but Angela didn't think love was play. She'd recently been in love, unsuccessfully and on a scale that made what she'd always thought of as love seem like a toy model. Peter Jackman had turned her away—permanently, she was afraid—from the types she was used to having take her out. He'd taken her to his studio. He was a painter who'd applied for a grant to the foundation where Angela worked, and got not the money but her, though he didn't want her for long. When her mind and her heart stopped reeling, she realized she'd made a vital discovery. Love was a discipline. It involved skill and hard work and endurance, and also a certain sense of style. On the other hand, love was well known to be a gamble, and her father was a gambler—the kind who gambled with money. Gambling had put him where he was now, in a sanitarium. He'd overreached himself and had a nervous breakdown. Money and love and happiness, thought Angela. They were related in a way you couldn't afford to dismiss, no matter how rich or how high-minded you were.

"It always helps to look your best."

"For a visit to a mental hospital?"

Mrs. Ganley looked baffled and hurt. "There as well as anywhere."

Angela said, "I'm sorry." Sorry for her smart remark, sorry for herself, but in a way sorrier for her mother, who couldn't help seeing herself as the heroine of this situation or, for that matter, of any situation she happened to find herself in. It was her nature to do that. It was how she got through things or got over them, by living and looking the part. Maybe that was as good a way as any, as good a way as her own, thought Angela, who went through everything analyzing—for example, her father's breakdown. Sometimes she felt as if it had been begun, maybe even settled, long before she was born, but most of the time, it seemed to her she'd had some part in it, not a crucial part but not a negligible one either. She'd tried to tell him something of the sort, but it only made him feel worse, and furthermore he didn't know what she meant. It turned out he wasn't thin-skinned at all. Whereas her mother was as sensitive as a very young child. Sitting beside her now was like sitting beside a pure mass of hurt feelings. Angela said, "I didn't mean to snap at you."

Mrs. Ganley could brood for days over some trifle, but under the present circumstances that was out of the question. "Never mind," she said in a way that meant, We're in this together.

As far as Angela was concerned, they were in it separately, though they'd been literally together in the apartment that Saturday afternoon, two weeks before, when Mrs. Ganley found the letter under the door. While her mother was reading it, Angela was reading her mother's face, the face of someone who was perfectly composed because she was completely at a loss—unlike Angela, who didn't even need to be told, "Your father's done something awful." Her mind had already begun ticking off the possibilities. Had he stolen something? Had he killed himself? She'd come pretty close. Someone else's money was involved, and he'd hinted at suicide:

Dear Florence and Angela,

Nothing in my life has ever been as hard as this, but things have got beyond me and I don't know what else to do except leave you in peace. I myself am going to try and get into a retreat house and see if I can figure some way out of what's happened, but frankly life doesn't seem worth living at this point and I don't know if I can go on. I'm at my wit's end, but believe me, whatever I do, all I want is for the two of you to be happy.

Your devoted husband and father,

As terrible and sad a collection of clichés as you'd find in the worst dime novel—and probably every word of it from the heart. To top it off, he'd enclosed the dunning letters from the loan companies.

The train slowed down and pulled into Mamaroneck. Children in shorts began to race along the station platform, trying to get the first glimpse of their Sunday guests—the grandmothers, the aunts, the friends from the city come for a swim at one of the clubs. Mrs. Ganley leaned forward in her seat. "Look at that little fellow," she said.

Angela turned away from the window instead and watched what was, in the first place, more interesting to her and, in the second place, less at odds with her state of mind

—the two new passengers who were coming up the aisle. One was a woman carrying a shopping bag and wearing a print housedress and a black straw hat—a cleaning woman. The other passenger, a man in a sports shirt and slacks, showed the conductor a pass. Some kind of railroad employee, thought Angela, an engineer of some kind, not a conductor off duty. He hadn't the perfectly steady eyes and hands of the man who checked his pass. Railroad conductors reminded her of doctors, priests, waiters, bank officers, carpenters—all the various orders, high and low, of people who inspired your confidence.

The train started off again. Mrs. Ganley sighed. "When I think of our car!"

"I wish you wouldn't." Neither of them drove, but Angela had been taking lessons and just failed her driving test.

"Promise me you'll take that test again as soon as you can."

"I will." But Angela wasn't so sure. She had a recurrent dream where she crashed a car into a wall and killed three or four people who'd been standing there, and though it was stupid to take dreams literally, that one was at the back of her mind whenever she got into the car for a lesson, except the few times her father took her out. He was a good teacher, much more competent than the instructor from the school, but looking back on it Angela was appalled at the state of nerves he must have been in. The trouble was well along by then. He'd been way over his head in debt, close to the breaking point. Then he broke, like a piece of electrical equipment that suddenly lets off a sput and a shower of sparks and gives out.

"I never want to see you in the position I'm in now," said Mrs. Ganley, "dependent on someone who's not dependable."

"I won't be." Dependent on anyone at all, Angela said to herself.

"I still think Marilyn should be told."

Angela let herself picture the brick house outside Boston where her sister lived. It was a row house, the kind that was a couple's first house, and Marilyn and her husband had just bought it; they'd just had their second baby. When anyone asked Angela about her family, Marilyn's family was what she talked about. It was absolutely necessary to her not to jeopardize them, even in her mind. She said, "There isn't any reason for Marilyn to know."

"If I were in her place, I'd want to."

"There's nothing she can do."

"But this way it's all on your back."

Angela saw herself doubled over under something cold, black, slimy, shapeless, half plant, half animal. She shivered.

Mrs. Ganley said, "You're catching cold already."

"No, I'm not. Stop worrying."

But to Mrs. Ganley, worry and love were inseparable, and what was really bothering her was the feeling of obligation. "When I think of what you've been through and what you've done for me—who else could I have gone to and got three thousand dollars overnight?"

Week after week, Angela saw huge sums being given away at the foundation. At first she thought that was what made it easy for her to give up the money she was saving to go and live in Europe on. Then it occurred to her that maybe she was her father's daughter, with no more sense of money than he had. It terrified her to think that, but the real explanation when she hit on it made her laugh—it was so obvious. She'd given up her savings easily because there was no choice. The dream of travelling vanished, and with it went the dream's responsibility, the obligation to be happy. Now, riding through the beautiful summer afternoon, she felt as free as she might have in Paris or in the Greek islands. It seemed to her you could stay this way forever, and that it wasn't the worst way to be—relieved of a dream and delivered, or in the process of being delivered, from a nightmare.

They were slowing down again. The conductor called "Station Harrison," and Mrs. Ganley got up and stepped out into the aisle. Angela went on ahead, and when they pulled into the station she was the first passenger off, the first one to get a taxi, but she and her mother could have walked the distance to the hospital. They'd hardly settled themselves in the cab when it was drawing up to the gates of an enormous white frame mansion—the old-fashioned, expensive piece of property that outlived its private usefulness, had to be unloaded, and was turned over to this good cause. This appropriate cause? Why not? After all, what house was safe? Or couldn't suddenly turn out to be some sort of madhouse?

Mrs. Ganley said, "I don't understand it, Dr. Laszlo," and sat back on a sofa at the far end of the lounge where he'd brought her and Angela. It had once been two rooms, and a strip of metal, the track of sliding doors, still made a dividing line across the middle of the floor. Behind this half —what had been the back parlor—was a glass porch, but the porches around the rest of the house were all open, surrounded by cut-leaved maple trees that made a thick but ragged curtain of shade. Trees were something that gave Mrs. Ganley tremendous inspiration. The first buds and then the forsythia and the dogwood blossoms in spring, all the colors of the leaves in autumn, even bare branches outlined against a winter sky—like the poor twisted limbs of her brother Frank, who was crippled with arthritis—usually made her feel as if her heart would burst, but today so much sheer natural beauty overwhelmed her. Or maybe it was having just come in out of the heat. She shook her head a little woozily. "I simply don't understand," she said.

"Mental illness is a very hard thing to come to grips with."

Visiting hours were under way, but because of the fine weather most of the visiting was going on outdoors. They had the room to themselves and, looking around at how beautifully it was decorated, Mrs. Ganley couldn't help thinking out loud. "I'm sure anyone could recover himself in an atmosphere like this."

"We got the place lock, stock, and barrel," said the doctor.

Mrs. Ganley patted the fat, blue silk arm of the sofa. "The taste is exquisite," she said. When she was younger, she'd hoped to have a home of her own—nothing like this, of course, just a comfortable house on a nice street, a little piece of the earth where she could reign supreme. She was a homemaker. She loved the things that belonged to her and she loved looking after them—not that there wasn't plenty to keep you busy in a four-room apartment, but it wasn't the same as your own place. Still, she'd have been contented, given the chance. "I've been a good wife, Doctor," she said. "I did all I could to make everybody happy. I don't know what to make of this."

"Sometimes terrible things just happen in life."

He spoke so calmly, it might have been the weather they were discussing. Mrs. Ganley had the urge to ask what nationality he was. She couldn't tell from his name or from his appearance. He was tall, gray-haired, handsome, athletic-looking, above all businesslike, and she wondered whether that was the effect of his stiffly starched white medical coat or whether something in his background or temperament made him seem like such a cold person. She wondered, too, what his life was like—what kind of woman he was married to, where they lived, whether they had children. She imagined it all to be perfect and she felt that she must seem a pitiable figure in his eyes, but she wasn't pitiable. She was merely someone who'd been put in a pitiable position. There was a world of difference between the two, and she wanted to be sure that difference came out. You're taken at your own valuation, she said to herself, wishing again that Angela had worn her pink linen dress. She also wished Angela would sit up straight. She squared her own shoulders and said, "I'm sorry, but it's a complete mystery to me."

"Take war, take poverty. Who can explain them?"

That was the philosophical approach. Mrs. Ganley recognized the value of it, but what she looked for in people was sympathy. She wanted to tell someone all the things that had happened to her over the years and to have the person agree that her life had been hard, and then she would say yes but that everyone had something. The doctor had given her an opening. "Three of my brothers served in the Second World War," she said. "My brother Jack was killed in the Caroline Islands. As for poverty—we were ten children. My father was a fireman. I know what it is to have to do without things."

There was no change whatever in his face or manner. He simply opened a manila folder he'd been holding on his lap and said, "We asked Mr. Ganley to write down the story of how he saw his life. That might throw some light on the situation for you."

Could a psychiatrist be someone who had to avoid sympathy altogether? In that case it might be impossible to win this man over, but Mrs. Ganley could no more not try than she could try not to want to. She said, "The story of Mr. Ganley's life is an old story to me, Doctor."

"Then let me just give you a summary. He divides it into three parts. The first part, his childhood, he said was the happiest time. He said his family was very close. He also said they were well off."

"Comfortable," said Mrs. Ganley, "but not really well off. Mr. Ganley senior was one of those clever Irishmen who made some money in real estate. As for close, I'd say the Ganleys were no closer than most families, certainly no closer than my own." But that was putting it too mildly. As far as closeness or anything else went, the difference between the Ganleys and the Laceys was day and night. Thinking back on that and on all the trouble it had caused—the family parties that ended in bad feeling, the accumulated bad feeling that eventually amounted to a feud—Mrs. Ganley thought it essential to add, "As a matter of fact, the Ganleys were rather quarrelsome people, especially the girls."

"Aren't sisters often?"

"Not my sisters and I."

"That's unusual."

"My two sisters entered the convent."

The doctor's face became boyishly alert. He might have been a ten-year-old who'd just hit on something he could dash into wholeheartedly, and so it came as a surprise and a disappointment to Mrs. Ganley when he went off on a slight tangent, and the tangent he took was a source of embarrassment to her. "How do you and your husband's sisters get along?"

"We haven't met for years."

"Do they live too far?"

"No, Doctor, they live in New York."

"Then what keeps you from getting together?"

"It's a long story."

"Tell me."

But, of course, it wasn't a long story. It was simply, for Mrs. Ganley, a horror story. "About fifteen years ago, Mr. Ganley went into business with Molly Ganley's husband, Dan Coogan. He was in the restaurant business, Doctor. Six months after he took Robert in, Molly Coogan called me one day and said, 'Well, I guess you got yourself a mink with the bonus Dan gave Bob.' I said, 'Bonus?' That was the first I heard of it. Then it came out that Robert had been juggling the receipts. Dan Coogan was out some six thousand dollars, and somehow or other I found myself called on the carpet." Called on the carpet was the way she felt now. But why? What had she done? What had she ever done except take people at their word?

"Why were you called on the carpet?" the doctor asked.

"For not being a good wife."

"Who said that—Mr. Ganley?"

"No, his sisters. They resented the fact that I considered my husband and my children more important than going around to cocktail parties and spending the afternoon playing cards."

"I see," the doctor said mildly. "What about your family? How does your husband get on with them?"

Mrs. Ganley felt good solid ground under her feet. "We accepted him as one of us," she said. "As a matter of fact we lived with my parents for our first ten years."

"Mr. Ganley mentioned that."

"Oh?" What else had Mr. Ganley mentioned? Mrs. Ganley was beginning to be sorry she hadn't listened to the story of his life. It might have given her a better idea of where she stood with this poker-faced man she was talking to. Maybe it wasn't too late. She said, "I don't know what my husband may have told you about my family, Doctor."

"Nothing, except that you lived with them at first and that those years were happy. But that's the third part of his life. His school and college years were the second part, and he says those were happy years, too. He says he loved sports."

"I love sports myself. Years ago, Robert and I often used to take the children to a football game, didn't we, Angela?" Mrs. Ganley had been hoping to bring Angela into the conversation, and then Angela went and let her down—sat there looking as if that simple question were a conundrum it might take her the rest of the afternoon to solve, and naturally the doctor didn't give her more than a few seconds.

"Mr. Ganley divides the third part of his life, his married life, into two further parts. According to him the first ten years were happy—I mentioned that. Then he said there was trouble, but he doesn't say what caused the trouble."

Several things came to Mrs. Ganley's mind at once. There was the time a man turned up asking to see the apartment so he could make an appraisal of all their furniture—Robert had put it down as collateral on a loan. Then there was the time a policeman appeared at the door at six o'clock at night, as if they were common criminals. It seemed their old green Chevrolet had been found abandoned nearby; it was right after they'd bought the Dodge, and Robert had told her the Chevy was in such terrible condition that the dealer wouldn't even take it for scrap—he said he'd unloaded it on a junkman and even gave her a few dollars he said he got for it, but it was money he'd won at the race track. Worst of all was the time she was in the hospital with peritonitis, tubes stuck up her nose and into her arms, and the first day Bob Ganley came to see her he had to ask her for his carfare home. Only a heart of stone could fail to be moved by a story like that, but Mrs. Ganley was afraid that a heart of stone was what she was dealing with. She was also afraid that whatever she started out on might be cut short before she got to the point, and the point could be stated very simply. "Money. My husband grew up thinking he was a rich man's son, Doctor, and to this day that's what he thinks."

"Which reminds me, I wanted to warn you—this morning I found him ordering a box of cigars to be put on his bill, and I asked him if he didn't think that was extravagant, but he said it was only pennies for his family."

"Pennies! Why," said Mrs. Ganley, "if it weren't for Angela—"

Angela said, "Mother!"

For the first time the doctor smiled. It changed his appearance completely, gave him an almost painfully inward

look, a look that had something sightless about it. He might
have been a blind man with little to go on except trust and
intuition—no years of training, no years of experience, just
his own flashes of insight. "Angela looks like her mother,"
he said.

"Angela," said Mrs. Ganley, "is the greatest comfort a
mother could have. She's a tower of strength, Doctor, she's
a treasure. She's my greatest consolation."

He laughed. "You sound like a *real* angel, Angela. But you
look like you're a nice girl anyway."

"Nice!" Tears came to Mrs. Ganley's eyes—tears of relief. At last she felt she might be getting across. "I hope
you'll forgive me," she said, "but I never heard the name
Laszlo before and I've been wondering, is it by any chance
German?"

"Hungarian. This early trouble in your marriage—tell me
specifically what caused it, Mrs. Ganley."

If he'd asked her to mind her own business, she couldn't
have been more crushed. She was as close to breaking down
entirely as she'd been since the trouble started. She could
have cried real and terrible tears, the tears of a lifetime, tears
of constant setbacks and of constantly having to keep going,
tears of betrayal, of misunderstanding, of confusion, tears of
never finding any peace, never having any security. But
instead of crying she straightened her shoulders again and
said, "The trouble with Robert Ganley, Doctor, is always
money." The facts could speak for themselves, but Mrs.
Ganley wished she weren't having to give out her facts
piecemeal. She wished the doctor would spend a little time
discussing them with her. She'd come here ready to be taken
into his confidence, but instead she had the feeling almost
of being taken for a ride. She knew that feeling well. "It was
just after the Depression," she said. "Old Mr. Ganley lost
everything but a couple of apartment houses and some funds
he'd put in trust for his wife. Then he died suddenly of a

heart attack, and Robert took over the apartments, but they were a losing proposition. He went into the estate funds, and the next thing you know everything was gone."

The doctor closed his manila folder. "Money," he said. "That seems to be the problem, all right."

Agreement turned out to be the last thing in the world Mrs. Ganley expected. It also turned out to be the last thing in the world she wanted. What she wanted was a glimmer of hope. "Can you tell me what progress there's been so far?"

"The shock treatments have removed the pressure from his mind. Ordinarily, the next step would be psychotherapy, to get him to understand what happened, but yesterday I had my first interview with him, and when I brought up the subject of these debts he said he didn't think they were any of my affair."

"I have the accounts right here." Mrs. Ganley reached for her handbag.

"I'm afraid it wouldn't do any good for you to show them to me. He has to come up with the explanation himself."

"And if he won't?"

"I can't give you any promises."

"You don't mean this might happen again."

"Who can say?"

Mrs. Ganley felt short of breath. She put her hand to the collar of her dress.

"Who can say there'll be no more war, no more hunger?"

War, hunger, poverty—in the last few minutes this personal tragedy had taken on the proportions of the worst disaster imaginable, for what could be more devastating than the horrors of your own life repeating themselves? Mrs. Ganley would never have believed such a thing could happen to her. It was all a revelation, except that it revealed nothing. It was incomprehensible to her that she who'd had the highest ideals, and worked so hard to fulfill her ideals, should suddenly find that they counted for absolutely nothing. "I don't understand it, Doctor,"she said. "I simply don't understand it."

Mr. Ganley was a man of average build, but he carried himself with a stoop that made him seem frail. In terms of sheer physical endurance nothing could have been less true. Hardly ever in his fifty-six years had he been confined to bed, and he'd never been seriously sick, never disabled in any way. It was an old grievance of his that he'd paid health-insurance premiums all his life without ever having got the slightest use out of them, and his health insurance was of no use now; there was no coverage for mental illness. But Mr. Ganley wasn't aware of that, wasn't concerned with the cost of his stay in the hospital. His chief concern was to get away from the place as soon as he could, though what was uppermost in his mind as he came out the front door was finding his family. The doctor had told him they were outside, but they weren't on any of the porches. They weren't on any of the benches on the front lawn. He went down the steps and around to the side of the house where the grounds opened out and where there were a great many more benches, but also a great many more people. He was beginning to feel conspicuous, and he hated that. He liked to blend in with everybody else, and yet people who were like everybody else tended to get on his nerves. That was what depressed him most about the hospital—the sameness, the regimentation of the staff and the submissiveness of the patients. It struck him more than ever now as he looked out over the lawn— the scene was so lifeless. Then someone stood up and waved from the white gingerbread summerhouse just a few yards away. It was Angela. Never had he ever been so glad to see someone, both of them. They both looked good, they both looked nice. It felt like years since he'd laid eyes on them.

He was in such a rush that he tripped on the top step of the summerhouse and landed in Angela's arms.

"I never thought you'd give me a tumble," she said.

It was something Mr. Ganley could never get over—that this girl who was the picture of the girl he'd married should always be coming out with things he might have come out with himself. He didn't know what to make of it. It was nothing he claimed or wanted to claim, and if the truth were known it threw him off. All he could do now was give her a rough hug and a rough kiss. When he kissed his wife, he felt her stiffen, but he didn't care. He was happy to see her anyway. He was proud of her and always had been. She had an air about her, an air of quality, an air of substance. She was a woman with great strength—not as great as it seemed at first, though. She had no strength to spare. But she had plenty of style. "You look like a million," he said. "Sit down. I'm glad you picked a good spot." There was more than enough room in the summerhouse, but no one except the Ganleys had taken advantage of it. "And we've got the place to ourselves." Mr. Ganley was delighted. He felt as if he'd arranged things this way, though he couldn't have if he'd tried. Things fell apart when he tried to take over. He knew that. He admitted it. But this time everything had turned out right, and it seemed to have something to do with him, and he was happy. "Well," he said, "what's new?"

Angela said, "I failed my driver's test."

"Everybody fails the first time. I'll take you out on the road again. Don't worry, there's worse things in life than failing a driver's test." Confusion showed in her face just long enough for Mr. Ganley to realize he'd put his foot in it. He kept forgetting that he'd let things get out of hand and made a mess of everything, but in spite of that he was optimistic. He felt that whatever had gone wrong could be straightened out again if only they'd all keep their spirits up and if he could only get away from here. "What else is new?" he asked.

"Nothing," Mrs. Ganley said. "How are you feeling, Robert?"

"Fine. I'm getting plenty of rest. The food's not bad. They keep you busy enough." If he'd thought about it he wouldn't have said that, but he wasn't thinking. He drew back the coat of his gray summer suit, put a hand to his belt, and said, "What do you think of this?"

The belt was made of cheap tan leather links with a brass buckle, but from the look on Mrs. Ganley's face it could have been alligator and solid gold. She said, "You had a perfectly good belt when you came here, Robert. Why in heaven's name did you buy another?"

"I didn't buy it, I made it." Mr. Ganley let his coat fall closed again. Money. To him it meant no more than good weather—sometimes you had it, sometimes you didn't. He couldn't understand how for some people, for his wife, money was everything, though she'd have denied that. She thought of herself as a spiritual woman, but her interest in things of the spirit was like the interest on her face now, purely practical, the interest of someone for whom everything has to be concrete to be real.

"Made it!" she cried.

"It's therapy, supposedly."

"And I'll bet you enjoyed doing it."

Mr. Ganley knew she'd say that. He could read her thoughts, and so it never ceased to amaze him that in the thirty years they'd been married she hadn't acquired the faintest notion of how his mind worked.

Angela said, "I'll bet you hated it."

He laughed. "I'd stay in the room, except they make you go in for things."

"What things?" Mrs. Ganley asked.

"Things they arrange." He made a vague gesture, but there was no brushing her off.

"What sort of things?"

"Get-togethers."

"With the staff?"

"With the other patients. I only went to one." And what a grim affair, what a travesty of social life that was—one therapist playing the piano and another handing out coffee and cake while the patients sat around brooding or complaining, or some of them acting like fools.

Mrs. Ganley said, "You should take advantage of everything while you're here."

"You don't happen to know how much longer it'll be?"

"Another two or three weeks."

He couldn't hide how completely crestfallen he was. "I was hoping next week."

"We want to be sure you're perfectly well first."

"But how will you and Angela manage so long?"

Angela said, "Don't think about that."

"The main thing is you're feeling well," said Mrs. Ganley.

"I never felt better in my life."

"Then I'd like to ask you something. Do you remember how you happened to come to the hospital, Robert?"

Mr. Ganley frowned. He felt himself to be looking at a scene that was out of focus. By doing something or other he could have cleared up the picture, but there was a trick involved, and though he knew that if he made an effort he'd discover the trick, he couldn't make the effort.

Mrs. Ganley opened her purse and took out some letters. "I brought these along," she said, "in case you might have forgotten."

Mr. Ganley glanced at Angela, but she was staring out of the summerhouse at a group passing by. It was a strange group—a woman wrapped up in a winter coat, another woman who was crying, a man in bathrobe and pajamas and bedroom slippers, and a man who looked perfectly normal except for his peculiar smile.

Mr. Ganley said, "Florence, I don't think this is the time or the place."

"You have to understand, Robert."

He took the letters from her. Angela came to and saw what was going on, but she was too late. Mr. Ganley opened the top letter, a form letter:

Dear Mr. Ganley:

Five months have elapsed since we last received payment on your account, as a result of which there is a debit of $980.87, including interest at the rate of 9½%. If we have not received your check within the next ten days, our legal department will initiate proceedings against you and such of your property as will cover the account and any costs which these proceedings will incur on our part.

Hoping you will comply with this request as promptly as possible, we remain,

Very truly yours,

All four letters were virtually the same, but Mr. Ganley read only the first. The rest he pretended to read; then he let them drop to the summerhouse floor and put his head in his hands. The scene in his mind had come into focus: He was standing next to a bedroom window, a casement window, a bit small for anyone to jump out of, but that was what he wanted to do. He longed to throw himself out the window, smash himself out of existence, but he hadn't whatever it took, hadn't the strength, hadn't the courage or the energy to act on the longing. All he could do was take the straight chair by the window and keep banging it on the floor, crying dry tears, whimpering to himself, wondering out loud, over and over, "What am I going to do?"

Angela picked up the letters and stuffed them into the

pocket of her dress. "No more, Mother," she said.

"Things have to be understood."

Angela said, "Not now."

Birds were singing in the trees all around. Mr. Ganley felt as if they were singing inside his head, hundreds of them. He straightened up and brushed back his hair. The light hurt his eyes, and he had the impression that it was stifling in the summerhouse. He was about to suggest that they go for a walk along one of the shady paths when he noticed the doctor coming across the lawn. Then he noticed that people who'd been sitting on the benches were starting to head for the hospital. "I guess the time's up," he said.

Dr. Laszlo had taken off his white coat. In a shortsleeved shirt and striped tie, he was a much less imposing man, much less intimidating. Strolling across the lawn with the Ganleys, he laughed and talked in a way that was every bit as hospitable as it was businesslike. This might have been a magnificent but informal inn they were walking toward, and he might have been the owner and their friend. "Well," he said, "how do you think this fellow looks?"

"I think he looks remarkably well," said Mrs. Ganley.

"We've fattened him up a bit."

"I wish he'd eat as well for me as he seems to for you."

"It's different when you're in the hospital," the doctor said. "There's not much else to do."

"But we've been hearing about all sorts of interesting activities."

"Do they sound interesting? We certainly try."

The hospital porches were practically empty, but the hall was full of visitors and patients saying their good-byes. Mr. Ganley said, "I'll leave you here."

But the doctor had a different idea. "Just this once we'll let them come up part of the way." It wasn't clear whether he was acting on a generous impulse or a professional hunch, but in either case it seemed to the three Ganleys like a terrible idea.

Mr. Ganley quickly said, "There's no need for them to come up. It's too much trouble. They don't have to bother."

"It isn't a question of bother," said Mrs. Ganley. "If Dr. Laszlo says we can come up, then maybe we should. What do you think, Angela?"

"We have to catch a train," Angela said.

Mrs. Ganley looked at her watch. "Time is no problem."

"Then come on up," said the doctor.

The hospital had a little mahogany-panelled elevator that dated back to the time when the mansion was privately owned. It was the prettiest possible relic of bygone days, but for more than two people it was cramped quarters. The short ride was uncomfortable and awkward, and whatever the doctor might have had in mind, the whole burden of making it pay off rested with him. "They don't make them like this anymore," he said, raising his voice over the hum and creak of the machinery. "Look at that wood. Look at that work-manship. And it runs like a Swiss watch. Marvellous old motor. My father was an architect but his great hobby was machinery. He loved engines. Every time I run this thing I think of what a kick it would have given my dad." He brought the elevator to a stop at the second floor, and the Ganleys followed him out into a corridor that was an ugly contrast to the rooms downstairs. Here the windows were barred. The floor was covered with dark-brown linoleum, and there was no furniture and no attempt at decoration— no curtains, no pictures on the walls, nothing that could be put to some destructive or self-destructive use. The doctor led the way around a corner that ended in a huge door. "Here we are," he said cheerfully and took out his keys and opened the door; behind it was a door made of steel. He chose another key and unlocked the steel door. "Now," he said, "I'll go on ahead and give you a little privacy."

Mr. Ganley turned to his family and smiled, but his face was red and miserable. "Sorry it was such a short visit," he said.

Angela kissed him. "We'll make up for it next week."

Mrs. Ganley kissed him, too. "Good-bye, Robert. Keep well," she said. "Keep eating."

"Goodbye, girls." Mr. Ganley put as much affection as he could into the words, but he was trying too hard. "Take care of yourselves," he said, and his voice broke—not with emotion but with shock at a discovery he'd just made, and with the strain of having to conceal from his wife and daughter what he'd discovered, which was that he couldn't wait to get them off his hands, but that in spite of that, and all the more shocking because of it, they were all he had, all he'd ever have in this world.

Yellow Roses

T he minute the phone rang, Louise Gallagher picked up
the receiver. She was right beside it, sitting on the studio
bed, writing a letter, but no point in her one-room apartment was too far from the telephone for her not to be able
to get to it instantly, and she usually did. She hated that
sound. Now she'd only had to reach out, but she might have
raced the length of the room. She sounded out of breath
when she said hello and she sounded cross or nervous, as if
she were expecting bad news.

"What are you doing?"

It wasn't bad news, it was only trouble—no, not that
either; Charlie Davis, the man on the phone, was something
entirely different from bad news or trouble. He was complications, but Louise hated complications the way she
hated the sound of the phone. "I thought everything settled
down," she'd got in the habit of saying, "once you turned
thirty." She'd also got in the habit of saying, "I'm in between," and her answer to "In between what?" was "Everything. Jobs, countries"—she wasn't long back from a year off

in London—"in between twenty and forty, in between happy and unhappy."

Charlie Davis didn't let her get away with that line. "You're not in between," he'd said, "because someone who's in between is going from one thing to the next. What you are is in the middle. You're staying put." He often took that tone of critical concern with Louise. It was a carry-over from the days when they first knew each other—she'd been a research assistant at the magazine where he'd been and still was a photographer. At the time of that original involvement he was more critical than concerned about her, but this was seven or eight years later, and the circumstances were very much changed. For one thing, he was married.

Louise made a face at the receiver; into it she said cheerfully, "I'm writing a letter."

"Can I come up for ten minutes?"

She looked at the clock. It was four-thirty. She said, "Now?"

"Right away."

"Where are you?"

"Across the street."

Spring had come that day—early spring, or maybe even false spring, but spring all the same, and Louise had done a little cleaning. She looked down at her old red sweater, old khaki shorts, old brown sandals. Her knees were black, her arms were streaked. She said, "I've been sweeping around. I'm dirty."

"Good. Dirtiness is next to godlessness."

"I don't think I agree."

"No?"

"Take peasant devotion—the peasants aren't all that clean."

"We can discuss it."

Louise said, "All right, come." She hung up and went and

looked in the mirror over the fireplace. Spring, false or true,
wasn't her season. Winter was. She was like those plants that
have to have cold. Mild weather made her look as she did
now—a little washed out. She rubbed some color into her
cheeks and watched it quickly fade. She lifted her hair away
from her face and let it fall forward again. Any real improve-
ments would have taken a good ten minutes, so she went
back to her letter, but her train of thought was broken.

Waiting is an activity. It uses up time and eats away at
feeling and energy. Waiting is, in fact, a balancing act. To
stay poised on the point of anticipation in the face of the
universal knowledge that any given meeting can turn out to
be disappointing takes real skill and spirit, and the fact that
Charlie Davis wasn't there right away tipped the balance. By
the time the downstairs bell rang, Louise was sorry she'd said
he could come, though less so after she pressed the buzzer.
There was that to be said for living on the fourth floor of
a walkup—you always had the advantage of breath. The
balance tipped back, almost to true. She went out into the
hall and looked over the bannister. "Courage," she called.
He came in sight, carrying a big cone of blue paper. She
cried, "Flowers!"

In a burst of gallantry, he dashed up and presented them.
"I wanted to come by with them last week," he said. "The
day after, I mean."

"Why didn't you?"

"I was afraid you'd think I was crazy."

"I'd have thought what I'm thinking now."

"What?" He went and collapsed in one of the two big,
ugly armchairs by the fireplace.

"I think you're lovely." She tore at the blue paper.
"Roses!" They were pale yellow, and there were at least a
dozen and a half.

"They'll be nice tomorrow," he said.

"Nice isn't the word!"

"When they open out."

"They're heavenly!" She went behind the kitchen counter and got a pitcher. "Red roses mean love," she said. "Pink roses mean affection. What do yellow roses mean?"

"Texas." He lit a cigarette and got up and got an ashtray from the mantelpiece. "I don't think that jar is big enough," he said.

"You sound as if this were the first time in my life anyone ever gave me flowers."

"Isn't it?"

"Certainly not. I've had them all—gardenias, camellias, chrysanthemums for football games—"

He leaned across the counter and kissed her mouth. "That's enough," he said.

"Daffodils, anemones, to say nothing of the little bunches of violets."

"Do that. Say nothing."

"I've been known to get violets in the middle of winter."

"What did you do, pin them to your little fur muff?"

"Or at my bosom."

"What bosom?"

"You know perfectly well I have a bosom."

"Yes," he said, "I know perfectly well."

She filled the pitcher with water and stood the flowers in it. He was right; it wasn't big enough but it was the biggest available. This was a furnished apartment, flagrantly nondescript, and short on all but the necessary equipment, and so far Louise had done nothing to improve it. Except for the sheets and blankets on the studio bed, nothing there belonged to her and nothing there could have belonged to her, nothing matched her own definite personal style. She was like someone obliged to live in an uncongenial society, like someone detained behind the Iron Curtain. She turned away from the sink and said, "Once someone gave me an orchid on a little plastic bracelet, and when I put my coat on I forgot it was there and I crushed it."

"Was he crushed, too?"

"He was. You'd have thought I meant to do it."

"Maybe you did."

"Me harm a poor, defenseless orchid?"

"Unconsciously."

"Never."

He sat down again in the chair by the fireplace. Louise put the flowers on the mantel and sat down in the other chair. Between the two of them was a mirror-topped coffee table with a crack that cut the mirror not quite in half. He looked at her across the crooked scene and smiled, but even with a smile his face had a cold expression, the effect of his eyes, of their icy blue. Remembering how those cold eyes used to chill her to the bone, Louise had to laugh.

"Seriously," he said, "I really did want to come up the very next day. You made me so happy."

She said, "I'm glad."

When the lovers aren't married to each other and when love is to any extent actually involved, things can sometimes be simple and even casual, but only if the one who has something to lose also has the strength and determination not to lose—strength and determination, in other words, to browse, to give every evidence of good faith, but to make no investment. Louise had had just enough strength and more than enough determination to bring off the night he was speaking of in fine casual style, but his coming now, the flowers, the tension in the false spring air all suggested that he'd been serious himself or that maybe he thought she'd been.

"It was time we got down to business," he said, "wasn't it."

"High time," said Louise.

"After all those virtuous years."

Had he some idea of getting down to business again?

Louise hoped not. The false spring day had sapped her strength and weakened her determination. In another minute she'd be squandering hard-earned emotional capital. She folded her hands in her lap; her attention went to her grimy knees and then to his section of the mirror, which showed a serious-looking, good-looking man of about forty, wearing a gray suit, a blue shirt, and a dark-red tie, a man very much to Louise's taste, the man, in fact, who'd formed her taste in a great many things. *Don't wear jewelry,* he'd ordered that poor twenty-two-year-old girl. *Don't wear makeup—women are pretty enough without all that stuff. Don't be so agreeable. Think for yourself. Read Tolstoy. Read Samuel Butler. Try new things. Try frogs' legs, try snails, try Pernod, try anything.* Louise tried and tried and ended up hating herself and her ignorance, but from that impossible position she'd been able —thanks, you really could say, to him—to start from scratch, sort everything out, and come up with the person she wanted to be and had it in her to be. By then she'd long since left that first job, and the job after it, and the job after that. Finally, surprising everyone including herself—because she wasn't the type to do something out of the ordinary with her life—she'd become an editor in a publishing house, a good enough editor to work where she wanted, and now she was being choosy about where she wanted to work.

He said, "Did you pound any pavements today?"

"The extent of my ambition," said Louise, "was sweeping the floor. What did you do?"

"Went over the layout of my book."

"Is there much work to be done?"

"A monumental amount. My wife says she's never seen such a lousy job of reproduction."

Louise leaned a little to the left in her chair, out of the way of the sunlight that was streaming into the room. At this particular time of day—when the day, in fact, was dying— the light could be as strong as it was at noon. What was it like in Scandinavia when the sun shone at night? His wife, Karin, would know. Karin was of Swedish descent and had spent her childhood summers with relatives outside of Stockholm. Louise pictured an impeccable blonde girl in an impeccably Scandinavian outdoors, and the picture depressed her. "I suppose you'll be able to do something when they're printing," she said.

"I'd better be able to."

The mention of Karin also made Louise begin to dislike him and to dislike herself, not simply because he was married but because of the character of his wife. Karin knew what she wanted, and she wanted Charlie Davis. Though they didn't get along, if he tried to leave her she threw a tantrum. Once or twice she even threatened to kill herself, but, for all that, Karin struck Louise as much more admirable than herself or Charlie. "I'll bet you should be working now," she said.

"No, Karin is doing some sorting and numbering for me."

To want someone so much, to hold so fast and fight so hard—there was real courage and integrity, the highest kind of virtue to someone like Louise, who'd never had the conviction, or the stamina, the confidence, the willpower or, in other instances, the need or the desire to make anyone stay with her. Even someone who started out wanting that would end up agreeing it wasn't a good thing, though Louise never told him to go, she simply made him want to—want any kind of resolution rather than the indefiniteness she was so good at. But Charlie Davis had, of course, left of his own accord, all those years before. Then one day, after Louise had quit the magazine, they walked into each other—literally collided on Fifth Avenue. Though he'd got married, they began to meet for lunch. It started out as kindness on his part—kindness mixed with guilt feelings (because he'd been absurdly hard on Louise) and also mixed with wanting a little relief from Karin. And Louise's grudging acceptance of his kindness was mixed with a lingering desire to get her own back, but eventually the air was cleared. They ended up feeling more comfortable with each other than either of them usually felt with most of the people in their separate lives. But now passion had introduced the element of risk, and risk is incompatible with comfort. Louise was relieved to see him sit forward and put out his cigarette.

"Meanwhile," he said, "I've got a fascinating assignment from the magazine on the R.O.T.C." He stood up.

"You're leaving?" She was so glad that she made herself sound sorry.

He gave her a stern look. "I told you I only had ten minutes."

Louise said, "Well, whatever you do, go easy on the R.O.T.C. I used to have a good time in college at the R.O. ball."

"Don't tell me things were that bad."

"What do you mean, bad?" She got up and followed him to the door. "It was lovely. The boys wore dress uniform, and a special drill company went through maneuvers, right in the middle of everything."

"Thank you for the other night," he said.

She smiled. "The pleasure was—well, I won't say *all* mine."

"Good night, Louise," he said quietly, affectionately.

"Good night, Charlie," she said. "And please don't forget, someday we may need the R.O.T.C."

"Fascist," he called over his shoulder as he went out into the hall.

Louise waved goodbye and closed the door. The room smelled of cigarette smoke. She went over to the window and opened it all the way and stood there for a minute, looking out. In a city, and especially in New York City, back windows furnish a less lively view than front windows, but the precious flavor of intimacy makes almost any yard in

New York and almost anything that happens there as interesting as almost anything the richest or the busiest streets have to offer. People are themselves at the back of the house. Women shake dust mops, they water the plants, they brush their hair; children throw away their toys with impunity, watching where they land, knowing they can be retrieved; men scratch and stretch and often indulge in some purposeful kind of brooding—stand at an easel, or sit at a typewriter and study the composition of buildings and sky, so like a famous picture, so like a scene from some famous book, one that had cut deeply and surely into life and become a classic.

Louise's apartment on East Seventy-fourth Street had just such a back view of converted brownstone houses and town houses, though directly across from her was a small office building, a foundation for the cultural affairs of some Middle European country—she never remembered which country and always meant to recheck, because the sight of people going about their work was something she loved. Two of the windows opposite were covered by shades—storerooms, Louise had decided. The three others now framed small, pretty pictures of office life: A man answered his telephone (if only it didn't have to ring, if only you just picked up the receiver and found someone there); a woman with very black hair (dyed—even at a distance you could tell) sat at her desk, sorting papers; a tall, ungainly girl went over to a file cabinet, slid out the top drawer, and began flipping through the folders. Louise watched with not quite but almost envy—of the ordinariness of the girl's job and of her plainness. A plain girl learns very early on how to use whatever resources she may have. She learns what she can expect and how much she has to achieve and when she can conceivably take a gamble, but if a pretty girl is forced to learn those things (if she's not pretty enough, or clever enough, or sensible enough, or hasn't had a good enough start) then she learns everything the hard way. Louise remembered asking Charlie

Davis, in all seriousness, those many years before, *"Why can't you marry me?"* A fair enough question, if she'd been as charming and sweet and promising as he kept saying.

His answer—"It's out of the question"—was fair enough too.

Because charm and sweetness and promise were beside the point. Louise turned away from the window, picked up the ashtray from the cracked table, emptied it into the trash, and put it back on the mantel. The roses were beginning to open out. She put her face to them. What a satisfying gesture it was to give flowers, how beautiful and natural and yet somehow self-indulgent. Giving flowers was like giving a certain kind of love, the kind you can spare. The effect of the gift is out of all proportion to what goes into it.

Coldly, angrily, she lifted the roses from their pitcher, brought them behind the counter, and stuck them, head first, into the trash. A thorn pricked her; a tiny red gash showed up on her thumb. She put it in her mouth and went over to the studio bed, picked up her letter, and read what she'd written:

Dear Ian:

Your note made me so happy. It's nice to think of you looking for me in the Gardens. It makes me feel as if I may actually be there, or somewhere else in London. I wish I were. I think sometimes I almost am . . .

What rubbish, Louise thought, but, rubbishy-sounding or not, go and stay—if you followed them to their logical conclusions—were one and the same thing. People came into your life for good and all, for better or for worse. Whether they meant more or less to you, whether they played great or small parts, there was no getting rid of them, because they weren't really at your disposal, because the truth was they not only belonged to you but you belonged to them. You belonged to the hours of your days and to the events of those hours and to the whole company of people and things that shared them. And in the way that all men are said to have the same value in the sight of God, sooner or later what was trivial in your life and what was enormous gained equal access to your mind and heart. Her thoughts gave way to the image of a gymnasium. The walls were decorated with trellises of artificial leaves and flowers; overhead hung droopy clouds of white gauze; girls in evening dresses and boys in uniform sat around at tables of eight and twelve. "Atten-shun!" In came the drill team in mock battle regalia, medals from mock combat on their barrel chests. They flourished their rifles, turned smartly this way and that, stamping their feet as they marched, giving an occasional salute.

Louise got up all of a sudden and went behind the kitchen counter. The roses in the trash basket had lost their dignity but not their charm; they were mortified but ravishing. She picked them out carefully. There were ashes and coffee grounds on some. She gave them a shake and brought them over to the mantel and put them back in the pitcher. Let them last, she thought. Let them last as long as they could. Let them last forever. She went back to her letter.

. . . In fact, when I walk out into the street here, I find myself thinking the next street is Pembroke Road, then Logan Place, then . . .

What came after Logan Place? Louise looked up and was distracted by the reinstated roses—twice as beautiful, she thought, for having been humiliated; their fragrance twice as strong, their ivory yellow twice as fresh, twice as much of a lift to the sight and to the spirit. Eternal devotion! It suddenly hit her—that was it. She said it out loud. "Eternal devotion." Red roses meant love, pink roses meant affection, and yellow roses—Louise burst out laughing—yellow roses meant eternal devotion.

An Accident

They'd been making love. The big, high-ceilinged room was brimming with light. It was late afternoon but it was also late May, and you could still see the sun over the patch of New York City that showed at the louvered door opening onto a terrace. There was also a window, covered by a broken blind that was permanently lowered, the bottom resting on the air-conditioner and the slats all slightly out of kilter. This was a one-room studio, a sublet, with six months to go on the lease. The place was in disarray, but so was Louise Gallagher's life at the moment. It had served her purposes to take the apartment but not to take any interest in it, and if it offended the eye, the offense didn't seem serious on sunny days like this when the necessary architectural butchering—counters and dividers and shelves—bent the light into shapes that rearranged themselves interestingly from time to time. Louise waved her arm in a leisurely arc and said, "How do you like my light show?"

But Charlie Davis wasn't wearing his glasses, and all that light was a strain on his eyes. He covered them with one arm; there was a shimmery circle right over the bed, a second sun—no, a third. The second sun was on the mirror-topped coffee table, a direct reflection of the real one; the third was beamed from the table to the ceiling and shone down, all glare—like sun seen through a haze. He said, "I feel like something at the bottom of the ocean."

"Sunken treasure." She touched her fingers to his chest, one by one, as though she were pressing keys; he took her hand and kissed the fingertips, playing back the tune—a sad tune.

"Our last afternoon."

"Please," she said, "I'm feeling low enough." But these were familiar depths. She'd sounded them eight years before when she was in love with Charlie Davis for the first time and he married someone else. Now she was like a diver exploring waters where her ship had gone down, examining the wrecked hull, recognizing how unseaworthy it had been.

"I'm terribly proud of you," he said.

"To tell you the truth, I'm proud of myself." On Monday she was starting a new job—senior editor with a very good small publishing house.

He said, "Don't let it go to your head."

"I'm the soul of modesty, and you know it." He'd criticized her for that in the old days, calling modesty immaturity, but he'd revised his opinion.

"You know what modesty is," he said now.

"A virtue."

"No, pride."

She moved in closer to him. They had long bodies, both of them, and long feet and hands, long arms, long legs interlaced. "Don't be cross," she said.

"It's our last afternoon." The last of a couple of dozen; she'd been two months looking for this job—out all morning, back here by three at the latest. "Why shouldn't I be cross?" he said.

Why wasn't she? That was the real question, and the

answer was that she'd long since spent anything in the way
of bad feeling she could have had for him. Now she only
loved him, but it was a limited love, love without expectations—the idea of trying to take someone else's husband was
beyond Louise's powers of imagination or her powers of
anything else, for that matter. She was a conventional person. Though the conventions had never particularly re-
warded her spirit of acquiescence, she continued to consider
it unquestionable that they had the last word in life, and in
this case it was spelled out. A man who was married—even
a man with irregular hours, a man like Charlie, a photographer—couldn't go on indefinitely, or even very long, telling
his wife he was working at night. So this was the moment
for a break, and yet it seemed ridiculous. They were as much
cronies as lovers. There was great fondness between them,
a feeling so strong and yet so ambiguous that it frequently
ran off into foolishness. She pulled back and studied his face,
a thin face with a preoccupied look that was heightened
now, possibly on account of his being without his glasses.
"Can you see me?" she said.

"I can see you."

"What do you see?"

"A very sweet, serious girl. About twenty-two. Long black
hair, nice legs, a nice smile."

It was Louise when she first met him. She said, "You
couldn't possibly see her. You didn't know that girl."

"You're wrong. It's now I don't know you."

"That's silly," she said, knowing it wasn't really, for she
was no longer twenty-two. She'd learned what to give in love
—as much as you wanted. And how to give it—generously,
because what mattered in the long run was what you held
back. This was trickery, of course, and Louise disliked herself
for making use of it but she couldn't deny the satisfaction
it gave her to have mastered a trick she'd once failed at
miserably.

"You talk and talk," he said, "but what does it all add up to?"

"Five feet six inches, one hundred and eight pounds—"

"Skin and bones."

"—of Irish-American Roman Catholic." His family came from New England; his ancestors were Scots; he'd married a girl of Scandinavian descent. All that had given Louise a feeling of being beyond the pale that it took years to get over; when she did, she discovered she liked being beyond the pale, and she got a kick out of rubbing it in, but he didn't rise to the provocation she'd just given him.

"I hope you like the new job," he said.

"I'd love any job at all right now." She hugged him. "I'm longing to have an office to go to again."

"Nobody likes offices." He reached for his glasses and put them on.

Louise said, "I do." They'd met in an office—the news magazine where he still worked. It was her first job. She said, "I love going to work, getting a carton of coffee and seeing everybody come in and what they have on, what sort of mood they're in. I love the manuscripts and proofs and the mail and the phone calls."

"The roar of the greasepaint, the smell of the crowd."

She gave him another hug. "Please don't be cross."

"I'm not." But to be deprived of what you'd rather not have can be deprivation still, and this parting without the trappings, without the tears, the pressure, the vague guilt, the even vaguer commitment—it left something to be desired. He said, "You don't cry much, do you?"

"No, not much," Louise said.

"I can't remember ever seeing you."

"You must have—before." What an uneven match they'd been; how hard it was for her to see that and how firmly he'd had to go over and over their differences. For a start there was religion—he had just enough interest to be against it but not enough to be so much as an atheist. Then, age—he was ten years older than she. And experience—he'd lived with girls periodically for years, and she was still living with her family. And disposition—she was too good-natured; he felt he needed someone who'd stand up to him. It added up to the kind of argument a parent would have mounted and this, more than anything he actually said, made the truth so convincing and so agonizing for Louise. She said, "You made me so unhappy, you must have made me cry."

"I can't remember a single time."

"I can—the last time we went out."

"The last of the old times?"

"Yes." Neighborhood pigeons were roosting out on the terrace. All along they'd been raising a steady stream of complaints, and now their bleating added to the melancholy note that ran through Louise's telling of her story. "We had dinner at that restaurant that used to be on Third Avenue, L'Escargot. Across from us was a table of men having a night out. They were French, and I remember being surprised that French men would be out with the boys. They were acting stupid, and that surprised me, too."

"The French can be swine."

"No!"

"It's true," he said. "Don't laugh."

"I'm not—not at you." At least not entirely; if he sometimes went in for sweeping statements, she on the other hand had once swallowed everything he said, regardless. To this day, following some set idea back to when it took hold of her, she'd half the time find it came from him.

"A Frenchman who's a lout is a real lout. I learned that when I was stationed in France in the Army."

"I believe you," she said. Hardly any of his judgments that she'd ever tested failed to have some truth to them, but she'd had to learn to rely on her own judgment. "Anyway these weren't acting like swine. They were just a little drunk. One of them made a pair of false eyelashes out of a paper napkin and started fooling around with the owner's wife. Then they all began to sing 'Auprès de Ma Blonde' and for some reason that made me cry."

"Because you're not a blonde."

"*Blonde* doesn't necessarily mean blond," she said, "does it?"

"No, but maybe you thought it did. You were so innocent back then."

"And how you corrupted me."

"Anyway you didn't cry. You put your face in your hands, but when you took them away your eyes were dry."

"How did you remember a thing like that?" Louise was momentarily thrown off. Her own detailed recollection of the evening fell short of the reality he'd called up in one quick stroke, but then the reality was the suffering and, unlike him, she'd had to put that out of the picture. It had been her suffering. For a second it was hers again. She was suddenly back there in the pretty restaurant—across the way, the merry party of Frenchmen; on a plate in front of her, the specialty of the house, reeking of garlic.

"I really cared for you," he said. "I cared a lot. You just didn't care for yourself."

Too sweet, too easily impressed, and too easily crushed—those weren't grounds either for self-approval or for being thought of in any way Louise could conceive of as not detrimental. She said, "What else do you remember?"

"The first time I waited for you down in the lobby." At the magazine, his office was across a court from the room she shared with three other girls. One afternoon she was looking out when he happened to be looking out, too. For nearly a month they played the game of catching and pretending not to catch the other's eye. Then, one day after work, she got off the elevator downstairs and there he was, leaning against

the wall waiting for her, as if that were what she'd been
expecting, though she hadn't been conscious of expecting
anything. Looks across a courtyard—to her it was a simple
diversion, an end in itself. He said now, "You acted as if I
were a rapist."

"I went right along with you, though." Out of sheer
amazement.

"What does your new office look out on?" he asked.

"A blank wall."

"That'll help keep your mind on your work."

"It better. Paul Spier has the next office." He raised his
eyebrows. "Not that that matters." Louise was ashamed of
herself for bringing the name up—the man was a letdown
after his reputation with women, and besides, it struck her
as an act of disloyalty. But to the lover or the crony? How
much easier it was when they'd been one thing or the other
—especially the other. If she hadn't gone to London to live
for a while six months before, they'd probably still be that
other, still be cronies, but it turned out he missed her. When
she got back he was glad to see her and sweetly made no
bones about it.

"What sort of fellow is Spier?" he asked.

"A bit dull—not my type, anyway." If she'd thrown herself into making him jealous, she couldn't have done as good
a job.

He turned over on his side. "How many years have we
known each other?"

"1965, 1966, 1967—"

"Nine years," he said. "Think of it."

They were time flattened out, those years. They had no
definite structure, nothing that led to any conclusion but the
obvious. "Nine is a lot of years."

"Not the way we've been, off and on."

"When I'm working, we can have lunch together again."

"Now that you mention it, I didn't have lunch today."

Lunches were all there'd been between them for most of the nine years—nice lunches, thought Louise, happy times. She looked over at his tan gabardine suit coat hanging on the back of a chair. She liked the way he dressed. She'd always liked meeting him at a restaurant, coming in and spotting him. Waiting made him look more than usually preoccupied and a little apprehensive; it was his characteristic expression, that of a man expecting someone he'd rather not be meeting, and that the expression was no guide to his feelings Louise finally understood when she finally noticed that it didn't change by so much as a blink when she reached him. She herself had always been beaming. She remembered thinking that people must have taken them for lovers at full tilt, but anyone eavesdropping on the basis of appearances would have been disappointed. At that stage they were delving into what they'd only scratched the surface of before —the facts. They both came from mismatched parents, though very different kinds of mismatching. His father had been successful in business and a businesslike failure as a father. Her father was in the classic Irish pattern of wit and improvidence, and her mother was classic Irish, too—devout, innocent, good-hearted, fearful, a woman who was never clear in her mind or easy at heart. His mother's interest in life had been clothes and Caribbean vacations. He had one brother who drank; of the two others, he liked the older and couldn't stand the younger. She was close to both her brother and her sister, but they weren't close to each other; she was caught in the middle. Not that any of this was significant in itself. The facts could have been assembled in other ways, or other facts substituted—the exchanging was the important thing, the process by which each of them became the repository of the other's world, for these were facts that constitute the fixed in life, old coin as opposed to new currency, which tends to fluctuate. He gradually began turning from straight news photography to special assignments and then to free-lance work. She got better and better editorial jobs. He developed an ulcer. She was operated on for appendicitis—when she was in the hospital, he sent her the kind of get-well cards that are meant for children, with pictures of talking animals and flowers that had faces. By the time he was thirty-five, his hair was completely gray. At some point she changed the style of hers—he couldn't conceal his dismay, though he assured her that the two kinds of hair he liked were the way she'd always worn it (straight) and the new way (short and blown-looking). From what she occasionally said about something she'd done, he knew when she was seeing someone else and when she wasn't. And she understood that his marriage turned out badly. Every so often he moved into a hotel for a couple of days. He grabbed at jobs that took him out of town. He gave her advice along the lines of "Don't ever marry anyone who can't stand on his own two feet." The upshot of it all was what Louise eventually realized she'd probably wanted from the time she met Charlie Davis—simply to be a part of his life. It was loss you dreaded in love. Any kind of contact was better than nothing.

"Let's go out and see if we can get something to eat," he said.

"Now?"

"Right this minute. What do you say?"

"I don't know." She got a picture of them going into a restaurant, sitting down, ordering, eating. The picture seemed dated. "I had a hot dog before you came."

"It's no wonder you're thin." He ran the back of his hand along her side. "You don't eat enough."

"Yes I do. I eat a lot." She propped herself up on her elbows. "I like to cook."

"I didn't think you could."

"I like any kind of housework."

"You'd never know it."

Louise looked around the room. There were gray patches of dust on the floor; dust peppering the white surfaces of desk, table, chest of drawers, bookcases; dust discoloring the carving of the beautiful marble fireplace. "Nothing here is mine," she said. "I don't feel responsible."

"But you cook."

"Yes, I cook."

"What?"

"Nice things."

"What?" he persisted, as if this were something she'd kept from him, though the subject had never come up before, not directly.

"Oh," she said, "chicken with almonds, beef Stroganoff, chocolate mousse, quiche Lorraine—"

"I don't believe it," he said.

"Quiche Lorraine is simple. You buy a frozen piecrust."

"I don't believe any of it."

"I give up." Love that has nowhere to go stages contests that can only be in dire earnest or in fun—necessarily inconclusive but no less contests. She pulled in her elbows and collapsed on top of him. "You complain that I don't tell you things, and when I do you don't believe me."

"All right, prove it. Cook me something now."

"I'm not prepared."

"See?" It was a make-believe victory but it gave him real comfort. He took his glasses off again and put his head to the hollow of her shoulder. "How nice that nobody ever made you stand up straight."

She turned over, gently bumping him to one side. "How would you like some corned-beef hash?"

"Funny—I don't feel much like eating anymore." But she got up anyway. He watched her cross the room and go behind the kitchen counter; then she disappeared, hunting for the hash and the can opener. "Louise," he said. He had to wait for her to find the things and to look up, and then he had to wait for her full attention; he waited a minute more, for good measure, and then he said, "How dear to me you are."

She had a sinking sensation, as of a just barely adequate swimmer who looks around and sees a friend going down— and no one else nearby to come to the rescue. She said, "You're dear to me, too, Charlie," which was true, but she had reservations about him, reservations he'd instilled in her and that she could no more set aside now than she could set aside the love. She fitted the opener on the can and began to turn the handle. "When I'm back here, I always feel like one of those television cooks," she said.

"That's what you look like, come to think of it—except they dress up a little more on television."

She lit the gas under the frying pan. "Start off with a low flame," she said. "Unless you're in a hurry, audience."

"I'm in a hurry."

She raised the flame and dumped the hash onto the pan; she reached for the pancake turner and held it up. "In England this is called a fish slice," she said. "I'll bet you didn't know that."

"As a matter of fact I did."

She leaned against the counter. "Once when I was in London, I used a friend's flat while she was away for a week, and before she left she kept apologizing because the fish slice was broken. I didn't know what she was talking about and I didn't want to ask."

"Why?"

"It seemed low-class."

"Louise," he said, "let's forget about the hash."

"Fish will always mean Catholic to me, and I thought that in England Catholic meant Irish, and Irish meant low-class."

"Forget about England," he said. "Forget about being Irish. If I can forget you're that, certainly you can."

"That flat—" She folded her arms on the counter, fixing her mind's eye on the cream-colored stone house, one of eight or nine on a short Kensington street. It was precisely the sort of image that prompted you to go off somewhere —the remote and picturesque that you believed to be the world, which it or any such image only was or could be insofar as you left it alone. Going after it reduced the world to those familiar dark streets, the cramped houses and cluttered rooms of your own private geography. She said, "When Diana offered me the place for a week, I jumped at it. I thought it would be so nice there. It had two big rooms, but it turned out they never got any sun except very early in the morning. And the whole place smelled of mildew."

"Speaking of smells"—there was smoke in the air—"the hash, the hash!"

She straightened up and stretched. She felt she could afford to relax and that she deserved to, having got them into these safe, shallow waters. "Calm down, Charlie," she said. "Everything's under control."

He burst out laughing and then couldn't stop. "It wasn't that funny," said Louise, but he was laughing so hard he began to cry. She felt a little foolish. "What are you laughing at?" she said. He shook his head, speechless, but a minute later he was wiping his eyes. And then cold sober, or sober enough, anyway, to realize what he was doing but not sober enough to keep still, he said, "Well, if you must know, I think I'm probably in love with you."

She had the sinking sensation again. When you told someone you loved how you felt, you risked yourself completely. The best you could ever do was make it a calculated risk; the worst was to let it out recklessly the way he just had. He'd regret that, regret it and hold it against her, which might have been all to the good except that it turned out she wasn't prepared to be quite that good—not yet, not so suddenly. She said, "I mustn't know."

"Why not?"

"I don't have to."

"I know that. I just thought you might be interested." She smiled at him. He said, "The least you can do is tell me you love me."

"Yes, at least I can tell you that." Maybe he hadn't meant it seriously or maybe she was meant to take it that he hadn't. In any case, that was the assumption to go on. "I've made a hash of this hash." She emptied it onto a plate and brought it over to the bed with two forks. "What a mess," she said. But a mess of her making was just the thing to restore the balance and retrieve the situation.

"It isn't a mess," he said kindly. "It's just what I feel like. What's that you say on your television show when you sign off?"

"Bon appétit!"

The can had been the smallest size—no more than four bites apiece, with one left over. "That's for you," he said, "for going to all that trouble."

"No, it's for you." She pushed the last bit onto his fork with her own. "Because I'm the hostess."

He started to laugh again, but it seemed he'd laughed himself out. He put down his fork and lay back. Louise leaned over and set the plate on the floor. As she was sitting up again, a couple of pigeons swept past the window, coming in so close that the shadows of their wingspread made the room darken. The light being diffuse, the effect was flickering and also subtly menacing, as if mischievous and un-friendly hands were playing with half a dozen switches. Louise shuddered.

"What's the matter?" He covered her hands with his.

"Nothing," she said, but for the first time all afternoon she had a sense of things ending. It came with a jolt and with reverberations—she was back in the little restaurant on Third Avenue with her face in her hands and her life, as far as she could see, over.

He said, "Tell me what's wrong, Louise."

She stretched out beside him, carefully unfolding her legs, like someone after an accident—shaken, wondering what was the extent of the injury.

"Tell me," he said.

She said, "It hurts."

A Foregone
Conclusion

Something was wrong. Louise Gallagher saw that the minute she sat down beside Charlie Davis at the bar. He had a blank look, the expressionlessness that sometimes comes over children's faces in the aftermath of very good or very bad behavior. She thought: What a foolish business—this man is married. He kissed her and said, "I'm sorry I haven't been in touch." It was over a month since they'd met.

She said, "That's all right." The restaurant was dark and cool, a drastic change from the sweltering August heat outside in the streets of New York. Her head began to ache a little. Perspiration collected under her lower lip. She wiped it with one finger.

He said, "Would you like a drink here or inside?"

"How long do we have to wait for a table?"

His attention went past her. "It looks as if we don't."

She turned in time to see the headwaiter motion to a tall man with black hair who was talking to the woman at the cashier's desk. The tall man then beckoned to them, and they left the bar. Louise said, "Has this place changed hands?"

"What makes you think so?"

"The man with the black hair acts like the owner but he usedn't to be."

"No, the guy with the glasses was."

"The one who looked like Sartre."

They reached the restaurant proper, a narrow room with two rows of banquettes, a single row of round tables down the center, and four cozy corner tables set into booths, one of which was now empty. But the booths seated six; the headwaiter pulled the table away from a banquette. Charlie said to Louise, "I'd rather have the corner, wouldn't you?" She smiled. He was a dry, studious-looking man but he had a romantic nature, he was subject to flights of gallantry—sudden declarations of feeling, kisses in the street. "Can we have the booth?" he asked the headwaiter, who bowed obligingly and led them to the table in the corner. They slid in from either side. Louise dropped the strap of her bag from her shoulder and looked around. It was a very pleasant restaurant in the East Sixties, a location that had a lot to do with the pleasantness. This was a neighborhood of boutiques, of expensive doctors and hairdressers, of galleries and antique shops, embassies and cultural institutes. The publishing office where she worked was a few blocks south of the restaurant; her studio apartment was in a brownstone a bit farther north but within walking distance. This was her neighborhood, though at the moment that fact wasn't the reassurance it might have been. Something was wrong, something was different. She folded her hands on the table and waited to find out what.

He said, "I'm really sorry I didn't call when I told you I would."

She said, "Don't be silly." I'll call you next week, or next month, or tomorrow—it was a formula, a convention to be observed, not a promise to be kept.

"I got tied up."

A waiter appeared at their table. He was a very short, very thin, very young man wearing a big maroon bow tie that set off his long, pointed features and gave him an air of audacity that he perhaps prided himself on. He greeted them impassively, appraisingly, *"Bonjour,"* and stood poised, pencil and pad ready. "Would you care for a cocktail?"

Louise said, "I'd like a glass of white wine."

"And I'll have another martini."

The boy wrote down the order and handed them each a menu. Le Provençal, read the long flowing script at the top of the page, but it could have been any of half a dozen places. The Café de Paris, Le Mont Saint Michel, L'Escargot, Le Vert Galant, Ginetta's—they formed a single backdrop for this love affair that didn't end six years before with his marriage, nor with anything in the natural course of events that had happened since. Louise met other men, they both began to be successful at their work, she travelled a bit, his marriage went from satisfactory to bad and from bad to worse, but through all these events, impervious to them, ran this affair that she thought of as love *à la française*—wicked and harmless, hopeless and happy, lacking a solid framework and yet somehow surviving. Survival, she'd learned, was a question of a cool head and a light touch. The boy came with their drinks and ran off again. She said, "That woman over there in the white hat sold me the dress I have on."

He raised his glass. "To the lady in the white hat."

The dress was blue-and-white striped seersucker with vertical bands of white lace on the bodice. Louise thought she and that dress suited each other—both reasonably serviceable, reasonably decorative, making no great claims, aiming simply to please. She said, "It's a nice dress, isn't it?"

"It's a splendid dress. You're a splendid girl." He reached into his pocket; then he took her hand and put something there, folding the fingers closed. "You should have had this a while ago." She opened her hand. In the palm lay a ring.

It looked like a child's ring. "It was my grandmother's," he said. "I told you I wanted to give it to you. Remember?"

She hadn't so much forgotten as dismissed the idea as inappropriate. Rings belonged to explicit loves, loves with a context and a direction, but theirs, for all its durability, was an inconclusive affair. That they should go on indefinitely the way they were seemed unlikely, but that they should part seemed unnecessary, and anything else was out of the question since Louise was Catholic. But above and beyond that, this ulterior life they'd drifted into had become intrinsic to the idea each of them had of the other, which made the ring, to Louise's way of thinking, a great mistake.

He said, "If I hadn't had so much on my mind, you'd have got it a couple of weeks ago."

"It's lovely having it now." She slipped it provisionally on the little finger of her right hand where it was way too big.

"Things got fouled up," he said. "That's why I didn't call."

"I figured you were off on assignment." He was a news photographer; he was often called away suddenly.

He said, "No, my wife had to go into the hospital."

Ah, she thought, that was it, that was the something wrong. He'd had a brush with death—or at least mortality. She felt its cold shadow glide across her own life. "What was the trouble?" she asked.

"She found a lump on her breast. It turned out to be nothing, but the doctor put her right into Saint Clare's."

Sympathy and resentment welled up in Louise, cancelling each other out. For that matter, neither sympathy nor resentment was the right note, but neither was the flat note she did manage to strike. "When was this?"

"Three weeks ago. She was in the hospital for nearly a week, and then she had to stay home for another week."

One week in the hospital, one week at home, one week more for the sake of decency, and now this lunch. Louise

picked up the menu. It was a shabby business, she thought
—lunch with a married man. It was shabby and foolish and
maybe not even harmless.

"Do you see anything you like?" he asked.

Blanquette de veau, Crèpes Florentine, Bouillabaisse—
the thought of that rich food turned her stomach, but there
wasn't really time for a full-scale meal, anyway. This was to
be a quick lunch. He had an appointment at two-thirty, and
it was a quarter past one now. She said, "I'll have an omelet."

"What kind?"

"A plain omelet."

The little French boy materialized and waited, focussing
his attention on the map of the *Côte d'Azur* on the wall
beside them.

"A plain omelet for the lady," said Charlie Davis.

"Salade, madame?" asked the boy.

Louise said, "No, thank you."

"And *monsieur?"*

With a not perfectly straight face, he asked, "Is the English sole really English?"

The young waiter took the question seriously, took it as
an insult. He straightened his shoulders and said coldly,
"Oui, sole Anglais."

"You're sure it's not domestic?"

"Pas domestique!" The boy was adamant. *"Dovair sole!"*

"Then I'll have the *sole meunière* and a salad."

The waiter nodded into his big bow tie, collected the
menus, and left.

Louise said, "He can't be seventeen."

"Sure he can—it's all right with me."

Sickness and death form a paradoxically charmed circle
inside which all emotion has a fantastic quality. To be outside the circle is to be a bit prosaic, a bit dull. Louise said,
"Well, he's very young, anyway."

Charlie laid his hand on hers for a minute. "Are you angry that I didn't call?"

"No," she said, "I'm not angry."

"You look a little angry."

"I'm distracted." She said this, in fact, to distract him and with a glance around the room for inspiration. She hit on a table in the center where there were three women—mother, daughter, and grandmother, judging by the strikingly narrow face and the bright blue eyes that all three had in common. "Somebody's always celebrating something in this restaurant," she said.

He followed her glance. "That looks to me like a duty lunch."

"It's still probably a celebration for the grandmother."

"She reminds me a little of Granma," he said. "Granma used to wear her hair back like that in a bun." He shook his head as the memory carried him along against his will. "At the end, in the nursing home, there never was time to fix her hair so they'd just brush it back. I couldn't stand it. She looked like Einstein."

Louise said, "Poor Charlie." He'd been very attached to this grandmother who died six months before. A month later, his mother was hospitalized with pneumonia and never recovered; she died a year to the day after his father's fatal heart attack. All this happened while Louise was out of the country, living in London. When she returned, he gave her an account of each deathbed—how cheerful and sweet his grandmother had been, and how alert; what a shock it was to see his father helpless in the hospital, bare-armed and unshaven; how, at the end, his mother had counted on him: "I'll be all right," she kept insisting. "Charlie will look after me." He'd taken his mother's death well, but he broke down when his father died. Picturing this scene, and the others, too, Louise was a little at a loss. Both her parents came from large families, and when she was a child, an uncle or an aunt had died every couple of years. Deathbeds and funerals were as familiar to her as Christmas dinner—and as emotionally stale. Sifting through her memories, finding them not very sad nor even very horrible, she tried to embroider them for his benefit, but she soon realized that wasn't necessary. Corroboration wasn't what he needed. He simply wanted her to listen. And listening, she discovered that this man she'd always thought of as beyond anything so humble as family feeling was bound to his past by sentiments that made her own family ties seem casual, though she saw her parents regularly and was good friends with her brother and her sister. Above all, he was a man for whom things, to be real, had to be told.

"I hope I've seen the last of hospitals for a while," he now said grimly; but then he smiled. "The day I took my wife in was a Friday. We went to a Chinese restaurant for lunch, and she had sweet and sour pork. I said, 'What do you think you're doing? You can't go into a Catholic hospital on a Friday with meat on your breath!' "

In a way, the joke was on Louise, the Catholic. She said, "Catholics don't fast on Friday any more. I mean abstain."

"Then why do you?"

This was a Friday. She said, "Out of habit, I suppose." She changed her mind. "No, loyalty, really." The waiter came with their order. Habit or virtue, it surely made no sense to be digging into an omelet on Friday with a married man, or rather to start picking at it—she was genuinely distracted now. "Nuns make good nurses," she said.

"They weren't much in evidence at Saint Clare's. The place was full of holy statues, though."

"Well, sure."

"It struck me as a little depressing if you were sick."

"Maybe it's a help."

"Plaster Virgins? Bleeding Sacred Hearts?"

Aesthetically offensive those images might be, but they

offered a comfort that Louise was unwilling to repudiate, though she was also reluctant to defend it. She changed the subject. "How's your Dover sole?"

"Domestic," he said. "How's your omelet?"

"Fine."

"You're not eating."

"Yes, I am." She took another bite. The omelet was a little dry, a little tough. She drank some wine.

He was watching her. He waited till she set down her glass; then he said, "Are you sure you're not angry with me?"

"I will be if you keep asking."

"You are. You're mad."

She sat back. This was the moment when you thrashed things out, set things straight, cleared the air. How solid those clichés sounded, how well they appeared to serve the people who used them, and all sorts of people did—most people, it seemed to Louise. She looked around. The world was made up of a great variety of people, and that was a cliché, too, but it was true. There were people who had lunch with their mothers and grandmothers, people who had lunch with clients, people who lunched in solitary splendor, people who dieted, people who feasted. It struck her that she wasn't any of those kinds of people, but neither was she the kind to have lunch with a married man, and yet here she was. How had it happened? She imagined herself putting the question to the company, and she imagined the reaction. The woman who'd sold her the dress she was wearing would have frowned and declared her too thin; the little French waiter, with a shrug—too polite. Willful, the grandmother at the center table might have said; perverse, the mother; and the daughter—probably that she was silly. Louise couldn't quarrel with the view of the situation thus presented, and she could add to it only this: She'd once loved Charlie Davis with her whole heart and soul, loved him madly. Now she loved him dearly, but her heart and soul still bore the impression of that earlier love, and so, it seemed, did his. To be loved to distraction is burdensome, but when the distraction subsides the love can be gratifying, even important. He was the one who initiated their meetings, but Louise was only too happy to go along. She trusted him. He respected her judgment. They were concerned about each other, interested in each other. It was as simple as that. There was no such thing between them as defection; neither was there anything to have out or get straight. They knew where they stood with each other and they stood slightly apart, and that was all right with her. Then why, she wondered, did the sight of the mother and daughter and grandmother in the center of the restaurant suddenly make her feel sorry for herself? The three women were choosing their dessert from the cart which the owner himself had wheeled over to their table. Skillfully he served up the mocha *éclair*, the *crème caramel*, the strawberry *mousse*. Louise sat forward again. "I know who that man is," she said.

"Which man?"

"The new owner. He used to run Ginetta's."

"He's gone up in the world then."

Ginetta's was the first of their restaurants, a cheap café within walking distance of the office where they'd both worked, but far enough away so that they weren't likely to run into people they knew. To invoke it now was to invoke the spirit of that other time, the intoxicating spirit of intrigue.

He said, "I never know how much I miss you till I see you."

Louise said, "Me, too."

"You don't know how much I miss you till I see you?"

"You know what I mean."

She was still avoiding the issue, but he let it pass. He wasn't really in the mood to quibble or to beat around the bush. He said, "I wish I didn't have an appointment this afternoon, and I wish you had the afternoon off." He reached for her hand. "Or let me put it another way: Why don't I cancel my appointment? And why don't you call in and say something's come up?" There was a gentle, serious expression on his face. It was Louise who looked blank, as if she were the one who'd had a brush with death, whose feelings were taken up elsewhere, leaving hardly anything for the moment at hand.

"I'm up to my eyes in authors," she said.

He let go of her hand. She pushed her plate away. The little French boy sprang forward—the peak of the lunch hour was past; he and the other waiters were anxious to start clearing the tables and setting them up again for dinner. *"Fini?"* he asked.

Louise said, "Yes."

"Fini, monsieur?"

"Fini," said Charlie.

The waiter took away the plates and returned with a menu. Louise said, "No dessert for me, thank you."

"Café?" the waiter asked.

She shook her head. "I still have some of my wine."

"Monsieur?"

"Coffee for me. And I guess we'd better have the bill."

When the boy was gone, Charlie reached for her hand again. As there was never any real reason for them to quarrel, neither were there ever any grounds for hard feelings. He turned the little ring so that it faced up. "They're opals," he said.

She took her first good look at it. The setting was pink gold, the three small stones were surrounded by diamond chips. What did it represent? Afternoons in bed, lunches in restaurants, kisses in the street—the bright side of love. But what about the other side, the side that had to do with sickness and hospitals, bills and responsibility, houses,

housekeeping, domesticity, family life, the generations unfolding and bequeathing over and over the tokens of love
and hope—the dishes and furniture and jewelry, the letters
and the photographs. Without those tokens how could you
have faith in the love, or persist in the hope?

He said, "It's not valuable, you know."

She said, "I love it. I love having it." But there was no
way of reconciling this ring with what rings were meant to
stand for.

The waiter brought the coffee and a plate with the check
on it. Charlie picked up the check and studied it; then he
took two ten dollar bills from his wallet, placed them on the
plate with the check, and had a sip of his coffee. "I don't
know why I ordered this," he said, glancing at his watch. "I
don't have time to drink it." He wiped his mouth and
dropped his napkin on the table. "All set?" he asked.

"All set." As they slid from the booth, squeezing against
each other, she put her arm around him and hugged him;
at the same time, she slid the ring from her finger into his
coat pocket.

The little French boy was standing at attention. *"Au
revoir, madame,"* he said distantly. *"Au revoir, monsieur."*

"Au revoir," said the new owner of the restaurant. The
bartender waved to them.

"Au revoir!" sang the woman at the cashier's desk.

Outside the restaurant there was a traffic jam. As they
stepped onto the sidewalk, a taxi driver began honking his
horn, and the irritation was contagious. The short street was
suddenly full of noise and anger. They shook their heads,
dazed by the racket and by the broad daylight, the terrible
heat. "Can I give you a lift?" he yelled. "I'm taking a cab."

"No thanks," she shouted. "It'll be quicker walking."

"Where the hell am I supposed to be? I wrote the address
down somewhere." He reached into his coat pocket and felt
around there. Louise saw his hand stop and grasp something,

and she began to back away. He took the ring out of his pocket and stared at her. "What *is* this?" She saw his mouth form the words, but she couldn't hear them. Then the traffic began to move; the noise in the street stopped abruptly, and he repeated the question, making it more explicit. "What is this—goodbye?"

Louise hesitated. She couldn't keep the ring—she'd meant no more than that and so she was surprised to discover that her gesture, like the ring itself, had a meaning of its own, a meaning she now recognized as a foregone conclusion that she was obliged not only to acknowledge but to act on. Though it seemed an irrational act, a senseless thing to have to say: "Goodbye, Charlie."

The Voices of
the Dead

They were a family that liked getting together. To approximately the same degree, they exasperated one another, but each of them also found the others agreeable and, what was more important, reassuring. Benedict, the youngest, arrived first, with his wife Isabel, their two small sons, little Claire Louise, who was just three, and, of all things, the dog. "Come in," whispered Elizabeth as she opened the door of the narrow glass porch that ran clear across the front of the house. Her face was framed by three long tin clamps fastening deep waves. "Come in," she repeated. "You're early, aren't you? Mama just woke up."

"It only took fifty minutes this morning," said Benedict, rubbing his hands together. "Door to door." The timing of the trip from Teaneck, where he lived, to his mother's house in Mount Vernon (and, indeed, of any trip he had to make, no matter how brief) was of tremendous interest to Benedict, and he was continually setting new records for himself.

"Well," said his sister, "there couldn't have been any traffic at eight o'clock on Easter Sunday."

"Even so, that's good time," he said, slapping her playfully on the bottom. "Got the armor on, I see—the tin suit."

"Get out!" cried Elizabeth. She held the little boys, Peter and Paul, in her arms for a moment, picked up the tiny girl and kissed her, then turned to Isabel with a look that was critical without being censorious. "How nice," she said, drawing aside her sister-in-law's coat to disclose the tight-fitting mauve silk dress beneath it. "What a becoming shade. I hope you won't be chilly." Among the members of the family, it was felt that Benedict had picked himself a rare, costly blossom, and the fact that she became a Catholic when they were married had served to emphasize rather than eliminate her difference. "Why did you bring the dog?" Elizabeth now asked her brother.

"These two nagged me into it," said Benedict, knocking his sons' heads together, to their embarrassment and displeasure.

"I told Ben we'd have to leave her in the car during Mass," said Isabel.

"No." Elizabeth shook her head. "She can stay in the kitchen. Annie will take care of her."

"Could we leave the baby there?" Two heavy roses on Isabel's straw hat wobbled whenever she moved. "I'm a little concerned about whether she could sit still through anything that long," she said.

"Do you mean you've never taken her to church?"

"We think she's too young, and I especially wouldn't want her to be a distraction this morning."

Elizabeth put her hand to her throat testing a gland on the right side that was weak and susceptible to sudden infection. "Yes, I suppose you're right," she decided. "We'd better let Annie take care of them both."

As they stood there, three more people climbed the steps and tapped the top of the door, where two stained glass panes took the sun's few thin rays and cast them in scraps of colored light on the faces inside. "Good God above!"

cried Elizabeth. "It's Edward and the girls!" She loved surprises, and was so easily startled that foreseen as well as
foreseeable events could astonish her. "I stayed over last
night, you know, so I could help Mama get ready, but of
course it was made perfectly clear that I was only in the
way." Turning to admit her husband and her two tall daughters, she discovered as she pulled at the door that it wouldn't
open. "You slammed it too hard, Benedict," she said. "It
sticks every once in a while, and you have to be careful how
you shut it."

"It ought to be fixed," said Benedict.

"Of course it ought to be, but just *you* try getting Mama
to do something until she's good and ready." As the oldest
living member of their generation of the family, Elizabeth
felt keenly that the prestige of her position was in no way
commensurate with its trials, chief among these being that
they were always underestimated.

"Here, let me try," he said.

"There's a trick to it," she told him.

Benedict pulled at the door while at the same time Edward began to push from the outside. It gave suddenly,
smacking Benedict on the forehead, and then it swung back,
hitting Edward.

"You clumsy so-and-so!" Benedict cried.

"Why don't you watch what you're doing?" Edward answered. Jokingly, the two men jabbed at each other.

The group now filled the space behind the porch door.
Their bodies bumped against each other; their warm breath
hung on the frosty air, for it was a late spring, a cold world
for any sort of rising. Elizabeth said, "Come inside where
there's more room. Father Clem will get here any minute,
and we want to be ready."

They crowded in over the raised doorsill, the boys pushing, the baby stepping with exaggerated caution, the ladies
catching their heels, the men, after offering each other and

refusing the right of way, squeezing through the doorway together, like the children. "Put your things in the big parlor," Elizabeth said. "I'll see how Mama's coming along."

Two parlors opened off the long hall—a small one to the right and a larger one on the left. Over the years, the small room had its name changed from time to time, not because of the changing uses it was put to but because of various rearrangements of furniture in the rest of the house; from a receiving room, fitted out with a horsehair love seat, a couple of standing lamps, and a rocker, it had become the study (a desk), then the music room (an upright piano), the library (two glass-front bookcases), and eventually the television room (a large console set with radio-phonograph attachment). At the onset of Mrs. Nugent's long illness, a hospital bed was installed there, converting the parlor into a bedroom and delighting the old woman, who liked to be, if not the center itself of activity, at least close to it.

As Elizabeth pulled back one of the sliding doors to the room, she felt a flash of soft hair against her legs. "Who let that dog get away?" she cried. "Benedict! Paul! Peter! Somebody come and get this dog!"

"Crank me down, Elizabeth," called Mrs. Nugent. "I'm sitting up in the rocker for Mass. In honor of the Resurrection."

Before she reached the age of sixty, Mary Nugent had given six children to God—two nuns, one priest, the other three in early, tragic deaths. All her nine children had been consecrated to the Lord from birth (her sons named for the Popes of Rome, her daughters for those women among the saints whom she considered foremost), but she never expected that He would take them altogether, and the losses were terrible to her—the vocations no less so than the deaths, for after they entered, her nuns and her priest, in their black and white, seemed no more than snapshots of their former selves. Now, however, at the end of her life, she could say that if she'd suffered from this deprivation she had benefited as well, for at eighty-five she was a woman accustomed to religious privilege.

Her house was across the street from Holy Family Church, and as long as she was able she attended daily Mass, taking her place always at the end of the eighth pew from the front. Then, when her legs became so bad that she couldn't cross the street without worrying, as she saw some car in the distance, whether she would make it or whether the old limbs would give way simply out of weariness, she took to looking from her front porch at the services, which seemed, on the faraway altar, like the radiant miniatures in a stereopticon. In winter the images lasted only as long as the opening and closing of the door, but in warm weather, with the massive doors left ajar, she was able to make out the gleaming gold vessels, to identify each passing liturgical season by glimpses of the vestments—creamy white, or violet or emerald, or red, glowing like the blood of the martyrs, like her own bright blood. On clear nights, after Benediction, she always joined the voices, floating across the warm air, in the "Tantum Ergo," the "O Salutaris," the "Come Holy Ghost," and when priest and acolytes, congregation and choir were gone and the sexton had put out the lights and locked the doors, when the incense fled on the breeze and the flickering votive candles had consumed their own waxen hearts, she sat there still, setting up her prayers against the night.

But even that slight participation had been denied her, for now it was all she could do to walk to the first-floor bathroom and back to bed. Sometimes little Father Matthews from Holy Family came to give her Communion. Sometimes her son, whom from the day he entered she had always called Father Clem, brought her the Host. But without the ascending and declining rites of the Mass, the Holy Eucharist wasn't the same. She had to force it down.

"Take a drink of water, won't you?" the priest her son or the priest from across the street, who also called her Mother, would urge her, but she was of the old school.

"Don't tempt me," she'd say. "I'm no saint yet."

Rich though her life had been, however, no past honor was comparable to the one that would be hers this morning. Two weeks before, Father Clement had received permission to say Mass for her at home, and now the commotion was beginning. In the room overhead, Leo, the son who lived with her, was walking back and forth, his heels knocking restlessly on the bare parts of the floor. A draft of cold air blew in from the hall, and inside the parlor the dog, taking a roundabout route under and behind the furniture, arrived beside Mrs. Nugent's bed, looked up at her, and gave one long bark and three short ones, as though that were their private signal.

"Scat," said Mrs. Nugent, waving a weak fist.

"Get out of here, Queen!" Elizabeth cried as she entered the room.

Snapping his fingers, making a kissing sound with his lips, Paul darted past her. "Hello, Grand," he said. "Here, Queenie Queen!"

Elizabeth began to lower the bed so that her mother could get down.

"Here, little Queen," Paul said slyly and then he sprang at the dog. She escaped.

"Edward's here, is he?" asked Mrs. Nugent. She couldn't always separate the voices, couldn't be sure.

"He's here," Elizabeth answered.

"And the girls?"

"Kathy and Susan with him. Leo is almost ready, and Father Clem will be here any minute. If only my Betsy were closer by." Although her married daughter lived just a few hours away in Philadelphia, she was seldom free to come to New York with her three small children, and so Elizabeth tended to think of them as inaccessible, planets shining just beyond her universe. Straightening up, she drew the covers off the old woman and inched her body toward the edge of the bed, working the swollen legs, laced with thick, livid veins, over the side until she tipped off and onto her feet. They stayed that way, locked together, waiting for Mrs. Nugent to feel her blood circulating again.

"It's the heart," she said at last, faithful to her own diagnosis, twenty years before, of a fluttering sensation in her chest.

"Easy now," Elizabeth warned.

"I can stand up all right," her mother replied crossly. "Wasn't I the one first set you on your legs?" They pulled Mrs. Nugent's arms into the sleeves of her bathrobe; then, reaching the rocker with six swaying steps, the old woman fell into it, just as the doorbell chimed.

"That'll be Clem," said Elizabeth, snapping the clips out of her hair.

"My rosary!" cried Mrs. Nugent. "Let me have my rosary!"

Elizabeth put her hand under the pillow of the bed, brought out a gold rosary and dropped it into her mother's lap. As she turned to leave the room, Queen wriggled between her legs.

"Will somebody *please* get this dog!" she cried.

There was snow on Father Nugent's coat when he walked into the hallway—wet flakes, large as flowers, had clung to his clothes, clouded his glasses, and marred the smooth surface of the cowhide suitcase containing his equipment for Mass.

"Don't tell me it's snowing!" said the shocked Elizabeth.

"Just a flurry. It won't last." The priest's voice expressed such a strong wish for tranquillity that it seemed on the point of being anxiety.

"Everything's ready," Elizabeth said, "but Mama didn't sleep a wink all night, so she's terribly excited."

"Did you give her a sedative?" asked Father Nugent.

"I wanted to, but she wouldn't let me."

Just then Queen, who'd been sniffing at the baseboards in the hall, raced over and threw herself against the priest, jumping at his face. "I think somebody'd better get this dog," he said, with a thin laugh, and, relinquishing his coat and hat to Elizabeth, he walked into the small parlor. "Happy Easter, Mother dear," he said.

When she saw him the old woman crossed herself and then stretched out her arms. "Indeed it is," she said, "now that my own Easter joy has come!" Her eyes seemed pale with pleasure, but the explosion of pink roses on her print robe heightened the color of what was at one time a fine complexion. The day before, her thick silver hair had been set, and her fingernails were painted a rosy shade that while not flamboyant was nevertheless not absolutely conservative. At the V throat of her robe was a diamond bar pin with eight stones in graduated sizes. The priest delivered himself to her embrace, which was almost violent.

"Now, Mother." Father Nugent broke away and restored the part in his hair. "I think you ought to have something to quiet your nerves."

"Not before I receive my Lord," said Mrs. Nugent.

"As a favor to me?"

She clasped her hands over her broad bosom, the two swinging pouches that were such a burden to her now but had once been so useful. "I never have," she said, "and I never will."

"Not even if I insist?"

"I must heed my own conscience."

"Under pain of sin?"

Mrs. Nugent shifted her shoulders with a heavy sigh that was audible on the intake rather than the letting out of breath. "Elizabeth will have to get the pills," she said at last. "I don't know any more where things are kept in my own house. Elizabeth!" she called.

Elizabeth's daughters answered the summons. "Happy Easter, Grand," said Kathy, in her serious way. "Happy Easter, Uncle Clem. Mother's in the kitchen."

Over her sister's shoulder, Susan smiled at them a little too fully, as though she might be practicing the look for another occasion. "Happy Easter," she said softly but with great excitement in her voice. "Can I do anything?"

"Would you mind asking your mother if she'd be good enough to let me have one of my pills?"

When the girls left, Father Nugent opened the suitcase. His implements for Mass were neatly fitted inside, and he began to take them out and arrange them on the television set, the substitute altar.

"How would one of my tablecloths be for an altarpiece?" offered Mrs. Nugent.

"Thank you," said the priest, "but I've got everything I need, Mother."

"There's that lovely piece Aunt Kitty brought from Belgium. I think it would be nicer than the little bit of a scarf you have there."

"This ought to do," he said tactfully. "It's the standard altar cloth." Outside the room, Benedict's sons were dealing each other light, clipped blows that might have started in fun but were now delivered with real animosity. "All right, fellows," called the priest. "Later on you can do all the boxing you want."

"It's a beautiful piece of work," persisted Mrs. Nugent. "All hand done."

Father Nugent was relieved to see his sister enter the room triumphantly with a glass of water and a capsule that lay like a pretty stone in the palm of her hand. While she and his mother contested wordlessly behind him, the priest moved his lips in the prayers of vesture, skirting himself, layer by layer, in linen and silk, soft and stiff, embroidered and plain. "We can start now," he finally said to Elizabeth, who was arranging a purple afghan over her mother's knees, "if you'll call the rest."

They came through the door as he lit the two candles. Isabel, the convert, was self-conscious, having realized too late that her outfit was rather dressy for the affair; she moved to the rear of the room and sat down on one of the chairs that were placed in a row there. Benedict followed his wife, frowning slightly and holding her by the elbow; proud as he was of Isabel's beauty, in the presence of his family he always found himself trying to dim her effect. After him came Susan and Kathy, whose flower faces, under small, flowered hats, betrayed their discontent with this privacy of setting on a feast that should have provided, as perhaps no other could, an opportunity for publicity. Their father was next, holding Peter and Paul by their coat collars, shaking them and muttering, "Good-for-nothings! Lazy loafers!"

Leo was the last in. "It's bad enough having to go to church every week," he grumbled as he finished tying his tie, "without turning your house into a church, too."

"I know we have a surplus of servers," Father Nugent said, "but your voice, Ed, usually carries best." Recognizing for what it was this gracious gesture to one of the relatives by marriage, the Nugents watched with approval as Edward released the two boys and came forward to take his position behind the priest. (After Mass, Isabel would be given an apron and invited to help serve breakfast.)

"In the name of the Father, and of the Son, and of the Holy Spirit—"

"Amen," answered Mrs. Nugent along with her son-in-law.

Having Mass in her parlor, the old woman discovered, did not so much sanctify the room as make the ceremony ordinary; as she sat fingering her rosary it seemed natural for the Holy Sacrifice to be celebrated there. After all, why not? Many a set of vestments she'd helped make. Time and again she'd dressed the altar with flowers, always blue or white for Our Lady, white or red for the Sacred Heart (roses or carnations or great, big stalks of gladioli), and for St. Joseph—well, anything that was nice but not too dear. Her deep indrawn sigh brought with it the sweet smell of beeswax. I wish I'd had Elizabeth get in a bit of incense, she thought. That was the only thing wanting—that and the music. The sung Mass was much nicer. Closing her eyes, she tried to call up the sound of the old Gregorian music, but instead of a Gloria or Kyrie it was a piece of the Requiem that came, and she turned sadly to look at the photographs of her dead strung like Stations of the Cross around the walls of the room. The wonderful sons she'd lost! And the good husband! How fresh they seemed, smiling out at her, and how close—closer than the nuns hidden inside their habits so you could hardly recognize them, closer even than the living children there with her. Death took the bodies but left behind images that were never disappointed and cross, tired and unlucky, sick and even the unbelievable thing she was—old.

Her attention was caught by Elizabeth's girls, reading their missals. Well, that was their privilege, thought Mrs. Nugent. For herself, she didn't take to the missal. Father Clem had given her a handsome one with a mother-of-pearl cover, but she never liked to more than glance at it, though it was handy for carrying her prayer cards—the novenas to the Infant of Prague, and the Little Flower, and the one to Our Lady of the Miraculous Medal, which she'd made for so long that there was no telling where one novena left off and a new one started. Elizabeth used the missal now, too.

Mrs. Nugent shifted around to look at her daughter, sitting on the piano stool with her back to the keyboard. Susan and Kathleen had given her a thick morocco-bound book, but she didn't use it the way the girls did. She skipped around and was always behind the priest. Still, it was all the one thing, praying. The beads or the book. Latin or English. Aloud, the way Edward was giving out the responses, or to yourself, like Benedict there, with his hands joined over his stomach. He was getting heavy, Benedict was; he was built like her. Leo, so slim and high-strung, was the only one who took after Papa. "May God have mercy on him," mourned Mrs. Nugent out loud.

Father Clem, who had turned to intone "The Lord be with you," asked instead, "Is something wrong, Mother?"

"I was only saying God have mercy on poor Papa. I hope he's looking down from Heaven today on this great event taking place in the little room where we used to sit together, he reading his paper, and me with my sewing or whatever." Her voice trembled on the last syllables. You'd think it was a sin to say a prayer out loud in your own house, the way they were all looking at her.

"That's fine," said the priest. "Now if everyone will stand, I'll read the Gospel."

In his grave, cultivated, faintly British voice, Father Nugent gave out the story of the Resurrection; then he closed the book and smiled at his small congregation. "I thought we might dispense with a sermon today in favor of just this brief thought—we're extraordinarily blessed this morning in having the Sacrifice of Calvary under our own roof. Let us all try to prove worthy of such a privilege."

"That's right, Father Clem!" said his mother. "And if you don't mind I've something to say myself." Throwing off the afghan, she gripped the arms of the rocker.

Benedict said, "I'd stay put if I were you, Mother."

"I'd rather you gave me a hand than advice," she remarked, pushing to the edge of the seat. "That's the boy."

Mrs. Nugent brought herself to her feet and stood there, leaning on the son who resembled her so strongly that they might have been twins, one of whom, under some spell, hadn't collapsed into old age. "This is the most wonderful moment of my life," she began, "the fulfillment of my work, seeing all my living children who can be here gathered for this holy purpose. As for the absent ones—living or dead— God love them, I miss them." She had to pause—the little bits of nuns in their cold cloister, the handsome boys left in the cemetery gardens—then, pressing her lips together, she summoned back her determination. "This is the way we ought to be all the time, united in prayer and harmony. I'd like to see the spirit of this morning stay with us, each and every one, all year. Whether I'm here or not makes no difference, and I hope to God that when I'm gone there'll be no bickering and picking over the leftovers the way there is in some families. Elizabeth, you get all the silver and the linens and the good service plates with the gold trim. You know that. And the house is Leo's, to do with as he wants. Benedict and Isabel have the pick of the furniture and anything else that's here, according to how it goes with Elizabeth."

Father Nugent cleared his throat pointedly.

Leo said, "Listen, Mom, who's the priest, you or Clem? Let's get going."

"I don't need to be told my place by you or anybody else, Leo." The old woman dropped back into her chair. "That's all, Father Clem. I only wanted to say that we're a grand, lucky family, and it's a wonderfully happy day." Benedict tucked the robe around her legs and returned to his place.

"I believe in one God," Father Clem said.

Mrs. Nugent smiled to herself. They *were* a grand family, and she a very old woman. She looked down at her hands clasped in her lap, the fingers thick and freckled, like fat sausages. A very old woman indeed, and she hadn't lost her looks but given them away to this crowd of fine-featured girls and strong men and lively children—and to those others, who ran off taking their good looks with them.

Her gaze drifted across the room to where Peter and Paul had surreptitiously begun to pinch each other. Mrs. Nugent wagged one of her heavy fingers at them. The tinkers, she thought. Suffer the little tinkers . . .

After the Creed, the Mass was all downhill. The priest's voice lifted and dropped, sometimes splashing and eddying around an intricate word, but falling heavily onto the significant repetitions—"The Lord be with you; let us pray; forever and ever; Amen." Just before the Elevation, Father Nugent offered everyone a plateful of Hosts, which he said would be specially consecrated, and when the little boys deliberated over the wafers, their grandmother spoke out again. "There's no need to pick and choose. They're all alike." But the air healed quickly around her words, and moments later the simple phrases of the Consecration broke upon an atmosphere of reverence.

As Mrs. Nugent watched her son move about the altar she remembered how she'd once caught him in this very room playing Mass with Leo when they were youngsters. There was no playing about him now, she thought, almost regretfully. He was a strict priest and very particular, but even so, she couldn't help smiling up at him when he came to deliver the Host. Wasn't he the saintly one, though? And hadn't she made him that from the holy terror he'd been? With the Communion safely in her, she closed her eyes and worked on the papery substance, swallowing hard; when it was down, she let herself relax. The meditating always made her groggy, and, of course, the old drugs . . .

It was a soft snore she heard next. Her head shot up and she stared at Father Clem.

"The Lord be with you," he was murmuring.

"Where are we up to?" she demanded.

"The end," Leo said.

As Father Nugent lifted his hands to bless them, the sound of barking rose from the back of the house, joined immediately by a child's screams. Once more, brothers and sisters, nieces, nephews, and in-laws glanced around at one another, passing their dismay like a dish of peppermints. Closer and more hilarious came the cries—the child's crystallizing into laughter, the dog's clearly pleasurable now—until finally, jaws wide, tail beating passionately, the little cocker spaniel dashed into the room, Claire Louise hard after her. Snorting and slobbering with joy, Queen began to sniff the two young girls, who sprang to their feet, brushing at their dark wool dresses, stepping back and into each other. "Oh!" they cried. "For heaven's sake! Go away!"

As though this were no dog of theirs, Peter and Paul turned to each other and began to laugh.

"Outside, Queen!" Benedict ordered.

"Why didn't you leave the mutt home?" Leo said.

"Will *somebody please* get that dog?" cried Elizabeth.

"Bad doggy," Claire Louise said from the doorway, where she stood on one foot, swinging the other back and forth. "Bad doggy run away." The bold smile she gave them changed to a grimace as she was grabbed from behind and pressed against a fat chest.

Annie had come and knelt in back of the child. "God forgive me, Mrs. Nugent, but they got away. I was in the yard, putting out some garbage, and didn't she open the door on me and run off with the dog ahead of her! I'm sorry, Father," she said, turning to the priest and blessing herself.

Father Nugent absolved her with an uneasy smile and raised his hands again. The dog had crawled under the love seat, where nobody could reach her.

"Go, the mass is ended," chanted the priest.

"Thanks be to God," Edward answered.

"Elizabeth," Mrs. Nugent called grandly. "While you're over there at the piano, how about giving us 'Holy God We Praise Thy Name'?"

Elizabeth stood up and twirled the piano stool to a more comfortable height; then she felt her way to the proper key and struck the opening chords of the hymn.

Rarefied, already remote, as the voices of the dead might sound could they sing out, Mrs. Nugent's voice issued from her dry throat. " 'Ho-ly Go-od we pra-aise Thy name . . .' Everybody!" she cried, beating the air like a maestro. "Come now, *everybody* sing."

One by one they joined her—the two girls, who did really like the sound of their own voices; the little boys, who under ordinary circumstances didn't sing but now accepted any relief for their oppressed spirits; Edward, who was tone-deaf; Leo, who sang under his breath; Benedict, who hummed along because he couldn't remember the words; Elizabeth, whose great accomplishment was to sing and play at the same time; Annie, who sang through tears of remorse and confusion; Father Nugent, who went along stiffly—liturgically speaking, the old hymn was in the worst possible taste.

" 'In-fi-nite Thy vast do-main,' " they sang. " 'E-ver-la-a-sting i-is Thy reign.' " Isabel, who hadn't the same heritage of religious music to draw on, looked from one to the other and smiled, the roses on her hat rolling gently.

From under the love seat, Queen barked and barked again and then fell to panting.

"Hap-py birth-day to you," sang Claire Louise.

When they finished, Mrs. Nugent sat back. "Gregory and John were the boys who could sing that one," she said. "They were the ones with the voices." The memory made her smile sadly, and then she started to sing again. " 'Soft and the sha-dows fal-ling, on land and sea—' Come now, Elizabeth," she interrupted herself. "Surely you haven't forgotten this one! Many and many's the time you played it for your father."

"Why, Mama, that's no hymn!" Elizabeth glanced at her brother, who was standing, still vested, before the altar. "We're in church," she said.

"What is this, anyway," said Leo, "a Mass or a concert?" Reaching into his pocket he withdrew a pack of cigarettes and tapped one out, while in back of him Benedict shifted his weight from one foot to the other, mindful of the transplanted flower of Protestantism beside him.

As they all waited, watching the priest, his lips moved. " 'Some-where a voice is cal-ling,' " Father Nugent sang patiently—defying his ear, his scruples, and the encyclical of Pius X on the liturgy—" 'cal-ling for me . . .' "

"That's it!" Mrs. Nugent let the song go as he took it up. "That's it!" she cried. "All of you, now! All of you!"

The Perfect
Crime

It was a minute to three on Friday, and the ferry left at three, but it was less than half full. Later that day and all day Saturday and all day Sunday, if the good weather held, the boats would be packed, and most of the crowd would be on the upper deck, which was open, but now there were only one or two members of the flamboyant, carefully dishevelled, and, on the whole, depressing mob that landed on the island every weekend. For two days they cruised the boardwalks and the beach, sizing each other up, sometimes pairing off; then on Sunday night or Monday morning they took off, leaving the place to people who for the most part owned houses on the island, people like these who'd caught the early boat and settled themselves in the comfortable shelter of the closed-in lower deck. There were men in business suits, jackets folded across their knees, neckties loosened or dispensed with, a briefcase or a newspaper on the bench beside them. There were mothers in last year's blouses and skirts or shorts, back from the mainland, where they'd been shopping or taking a child to the dentist. There were pairs of teen-age girls, too young to have summer jobs except babysitting, who'd probably been breaking the long summer day by a trip over to the movies or the five-and-ten. This was August. The teen-agers were as tanned as they or anyone could expect or want to be, and for them the island in midsummer might as well have been Alcatraz. During the week, hardly any teen-age boys stayed on the island. The boys, when they turned sixteen, got jobs on the mainland, or the best ones worked on the boats as deckhand, one of three or four moody roustabouts who sometimes helped people with their baggage but were mainly on hand for hauling the bulk of the cargo, which was groceries. There was only one store over on the island, and its stock was limited and select. If you were shopping for beer, quinine water, bitters, cans of anchovies or sardines or smoked oysters, salted nuts, pretzels, cheese spread, meat paste, soda crackers, suntan or sunburn lotion, or aspirin, you were all right; or if you wanted milk, eggs, bacon, bread, butter, instant coffee, cookies, soft drinks, orange juice, hamburger meat, hot dogs, or dry cereal, you were still all right. But anything more, anything you could put together and seriously call dinner, had to be ordered from the mainland and shipped over by ferry in cardboard cartons that were always in danger of splitting or getting lost in the shuffle.

At three on the dot, the pilot pounded down the center of the lower deck, barefoot but impressive, the muscles of his back and chest pulling against his filthy, torn, and shrunken gray T-shirt. Since the summer before, Michael Stringer had let his curly red hair grow out. It was a burning bush around his handsome face, and when he stopped beside her Nora Barrett didn't know who it was until he said hello —there was no mistaking that low, rather sheepishly friendly voice. "Hi, Michael," she said, congratulating herself on not having first told him she didn't recognize him. "Are you up in the cabin now?"

The smile he gave her was like his voice, friendly and

sheepish and completely winning. "Yeah. How long are you down for?"

"A couple of days."

He wrapped his arms around his chest and tucked his hands into his armpits. "I saw your folks on the beach yesterday."

Nora was pretty and had an easy smile and the lightest possible manner that could be consistent with real interest. People Michael's age, which was a dozen years behind her own, always warmed up to her, and if she was in the mood she'd warm up to them, but today she wasn't in the mood —not after a train ride that took twenty minutes longer than it was supposed to and then a wild dash for a cab over to the ferry. There was no time for warming up, anyway. Michael said, "Well, I'd better get going before Old Man Nelson starts raising Cain."

Nora said, "I'll be seeing you."

At the bow of the ferry were three steps leading to a door. Michael bounded up the steps and into the pilot's cabin. Outside, another boy leapt from the dock onto the boat, drew in the lines and cast off. The engine started up, the boat backed and turned, and the seagulls standing around on weathered piles began blinking their angry eyes, on the lookout for any sort of a meal that might be stirred up by the boat as it went rocking out into the bay. As they picked up speed, spray was dashed against the windows, and the rocking became a hard bounce that Nora, for reasons having nothing to do with the physical sensation, both liked and minded. The feeling of getting close to where she was going was pleasant, but the closer she got to the island the more she mentally drew back. It was a place of jarring contrasts —a pure stretch of sand and water meant, you'd have said, to be kept in its pure state, but it lay close to New York City, and there was no holding the city off and no reason for trying to hold it off that didn't come from selfishness or hypersen-

sitivity or snobbery. The weekenders from New York had as
much right to the place as the people who owned houses
there. As far as rights went, Nora considered that her own
didn't exactly stand up. She was neither one thing nor the
other, not like the invaders—she was anything but flamboyant—and not like the settlers, either. Her family didn't own
a house on the island; they rented. But something else,
something related to that fact but also distinct from it, set
her off, at least in her own mind, from the other passengers.
This was the radical difference between people who are
rooted in life and people whose lives have been episodic,
between those who are single-minded and others, like Nora,
fatally attracted to the random. She looked out the window.
The bay was dotted with small fishing boats, each with an
enclosure at one end. She'd never noticed that particular
kind of boat out there before; they looked like sampans, and
made a pretty and faintly comical effect, bobbing in the
wake of the ferry, but the effect was smudged. Spray was
raining down the window now. Nora got up and went to the
stern of the boat, where a flight of steps led to the top deck.
Up there the wind whipped her hair into her face; she
turned, and her hair streamed back, and she saw two girls
smoking and talking at the far end of the deck, and a man
with a St. Bernard that was restlessly straining at a long
leash. Nora sat down near the steps. The sun was in her eyes,
and so it was a minute before she took in the woman sitting
across from her, an old woman dressed entirely in black—
black dress, black stockings, black shoes worn to a comfortable looseness. Her hair was knotted in a bun at the back of
her neck, and she held a cakebox on her lap. She should have
been crossing the Bay of Naples. Or the Strait of Gibraltar.
What was she doing here? Nora decided that the woman
lived in the town they'd just left behind, that she had a son
or a daughter who'd rented a cottage on the island and
invited her over to stay. But where was her luggage? Down-

stairs? No. Everything about the old woman spoke of few possessions devotedly tended. If she'd had a suitcase, she'd have stayed right with it. So she'd come with just the white cardboard cakebox tied with red string. Had she been invited only for the day? Could it be a friend whose family she was visiting? And why was she on the open deck? She had to tuck her black skirt under her to keep it from flapping, and she couldn't have liked having stray hairs whipped loose from the tight knot of hair and flying into her face. Though if she was uncomfortable she didn't show it. Her composure was complete. She was the ideal mystery woman, imperturbable as well as unreal, an apparition set up for the benefit of whoever was there to receive her meaning, which, like most revelation, dealt with essentials: You were born into the world, you lived whatever time you were given and in whatever circumstances, you grew old and accepted it and maybe even were grateful—grateful to be released from the obligations of having to please and to charm, grateful to be allowed to watch and be still, grateful to have a small outing on a beautiful day and to be able to bring a cake.

The old woman lifted a hand from the box and reached up to smooth her hair. Behind her, a long, irregular line of green was beginning to show—land, land of an unmistakably recreational character. Seeing the old woman against a background that was so at odds with the old-fashioned dignity of her appearance, Nora thought of those artists who'd painted the Madonna in contemporary settings to make her a more accessible subject for the people of their time. She was put off by the incongruity in those pictures, just as she was put off now. It was one more jarring contrast. She got up and went below again. Michael was making the run in record time. People were beginning to look to their luggage —the straw baskets, the canvas satchels, the duffelbags and shopping bags. Nora had a plaid overnight case and a padded refrigerator bag with two chickens and a pound of lamb chops that her mother had asked her to bring. The bags were heavy. She had a long stretch of boardwalk to cover when she got off the boat, and transportation on that side was virtually nonexistent. There were no roads and no cars except a couple of commercial trucks and the small fleet of Jeep-taxis that zigzagged along the beach or along a narrow, sunken track that ran parallel to the main walk. And the Jeeps were expensive and never there when you needed them anyway. Most people carted their things in children's red wagons. Nora set her bags down near the boarding platform. She'd told her father not to bother meeting her with the wagon; on the dock there was sure to be a flock of little boys with wagons of their own, ready to hire themselves out. When the ferry pulled in, Nora saw the little boys, but then she saw that she wouldn't need to get hold of one of them. Her mother had come down to the dock.

Mrs. Barrett seldom met the boat. The house she and Mr. Barrett rented was at the far end of this community, and the walk was too much for her. She was seventy years old and overweight, and after any kind of exercise she'd give vivid and probably perfectly accurate descriptions of the rushing sensation that swept from her stomach up into her chest and cut off her breath. But like most people who live sedentary lives she took immense interest in the activities of others, and in this respect the trip to the dock was worth the effort, if only for the spectacle of the big cabin cruisers moored there, fitted out with every imaginable necessity, like little floating homes. Mrs. Barrett felt there was something common about the boat people—the women all looked hard, and the men always looked drunk—but, be that as it may, they certainly had the life, she'd say. They were a sight to behold, those big, rough people sprawled out in the miniature lives they'd fixed up for themselves. Another sight was the parade of practically naked young people who congregated down there at the center of everything—the store, the club, the post office, the telephones, the hut that was the police station, and the garage that was the firehouse. Every time she passed that garage, Mrs. Barrett couldn't help imagining what would happen if a fire ever broke out on the island. The place was nothing but kindling. It would go up in minutes, and they'd all be burnt to a crisp. She saw herself and her family lying around, charred bodies amid smoking ruins, and she'd wonder if the island was a good place to go in the summer. But Mr. Barrett loved it, loved what he called the rugged life, which meant doing without electricity and automobiles, though Mrs. Barrett had to laugh at Mr. Barrett and the rugged life—he couldn't light a gas or a kerosene lamp if he tried, and he didn't try, thank heaven. His part in the rugged life consisted of grilling a steak out-doors once or twice a week while she stood by with a bucket of water.

If she was going to the dock in the morning, she stopped off for the mail, and if it was later in the day she stopped by the post office anyway, and studied the notices on the bulletin board—lists of unclaimed letters; advertisements for babysitters, for painted shells or stones, for apartments in the city; the lost and found. Even the little store was interesting to her. She never failed to be shocked at how poorly stocked it was and how items cost half again as much as they'd have cost in the supermarket, and she never failed to be delighted when there was something special—fresh tomatoes, lettuce, onions, potatoes, and, once in a great while, corn. She drank everything in and it went to her head. As usual, she was out of breath today when she reached the dock. She was also ten minutes early, and so she sat down on the bench in the shade of the control booth, watching the water, till among all the toy-sized boats out there she saw one pushing its froth of waves ahead of it with particular determination. That one had to be the ferry. Mrs. Barrett kept her eyes on the boat till it entered the harbor; then she turned to the other side of the channel, where there was dredging going on. The derrick moved among hills of gravel and sand with, to all appearances, no more direction than a fly on the kitchen table, and watching the dredging was about as interesting as watching a fly, but Mrs. Barrett followed it for a few minutes. She knew it was necessary to put a nonchalant face on things, though why that was necessary she didn't know. Her natural inclination was always to show her true face, which was the face of devotion as she let her attention return to the boat, now tying up to the pier. The gangplank was lowered. Passengers began coming off. Nora was one of the first. Mrs. Barrett got up from the bench, but she couldn't manage to get much further. People were moving their wagons into position and blocking the way; then a couple of dogs began to chase each other; and there were children running around with no one minding them. What if one fell into the water? Mrs. Barrett tried to keep an eye on the children and at the same time to get a look at Nora, picking a path through the commotion. Nora struck her mother as very pale and thinner than usual. And she'd done something to her hair, pushed it back some way that wasn't in the least becoming. These things upset Mrs. Barrett, but they also fitted in with her plan, which was to try and get Nora to take some time off and spend a few days at the beach. There was nothing like the sea air and the salt water to build you up and give you an appetite. Mrs. Barrett saw herself making big breakfasts of bacon and eggs and toast, big ham or lettuce-and-tomato sandwiches for lunch; she saw herself broiling fresh bluefish, making clam chowder, and making her baked beans, from the recipe that had been her mother's and was always a big hit. She even saw Mr. Barrett grilling his steaks. And all this was in her eyes, giving her an air of supreme expectation that Nora, who came up and kissed her, could hardly bear, knowing how far short of her mother's expectations she was bound to fall.

"Thank God you're here," said Mrs. Barrett.

Nora drew back and smiled. "You look great."

Mrs. Barrett had been a beautiful girl, but her life hadn't been easy, and in middle age her looks had taken on the kind of cross prettiness that disappointment can make out of the best features. But then, as she began to grow old, disappointment gradually gave way to the surprising rewards of sheer survival, and her good looks reasserted themselves. The girl with the lovely innocent eyes became in the end this attractive woman whose attractiveness lay chiefly in her warmhearted expression. Strangers sometimes came up to her in the street and told her how the sight of her had lifted their spirits. As for the butcher, the florist, the hairdresser, the checkout girls and the manager at the supermarket, the bank tellers, the woman who ran the stationery store—salespeople in general—they outdid themselves for her. They also told her their troubles, and she listened intently and gave them sympathy and encouragement and said she'd remember them in her prayers. All this was, or so she claimed, a mystery to her, and in a sense it probably was. She didn't realize that a readiness to enter into other people's lives is something out of the ordinary. Another mystery, though not so much to her as to her daughters, was her complexion. She washed with plain soap and water, and every once in a while she dabbed a little cold cream on her cheeks and her forehead, but that was the extent of her beauty regime, and yet her skin was clear and firm, and her color was fresh, and though her face had a slight heaviness at the jawline, that was probably due to the extra weight she'd put on over the years. Now, tanned and rested after a week in the sun, she looked the picture of contentment, and, knowing that was how she looked, that was how she tried to feel. "The weather's been glorious," she said. "Here, put those bags down."

"With pleasure."

Mrs. Barrett picked up the handle of the wagon.

Nora said, "Let me pull. It's too heavy for you."

But Nora, who weighed one hundred and two pounds, was no match for her mother, and Mrs. Barrett kept the handle. Though she was the stronger, she was obviously much the less limber, and she had trouble maneuvering the wagon. The going was slow and clumsy till they turned onto the trunk of the T-shaped dock, which was wider than the tip. There Mrs. Barrett allowed herself another look at Nora. "What have you done to your hair?" she said.

"I pinned it back. It got blown around on the boat."

Any deviation from the world of her own mind amazed Mrs. Barrett, and what she didn't anticipate she couldn't quite understand and didn't really trust. She said, "How did that happen?"

"I sat upstairs." They'd come to the place where the cement of the dock gave way to boardwalk and to the first of a number of gradual but very definite grades. Nora said, "Come on, let me have the wagon."

"I'll do no such thing." Mrs. Barrett decided to open her campaign. "You look dead on your feet," she said. "You've been working too hard. I can tell."

Nora was an assistant to a man named Richard Deck, who produced television commercials. She loved her job. She loved movies, even those base abbreviations turned out by the advertising agency, but she wasn't going to have to stay there much longer. Deck had taken an option on a book. He was going to make a movie of his own, and he was going to take Nora along, but it meant extra hours now, overtime nearly every night in the week. That Nora thrived on this was beyond her mother, who didn't know that she herself enjoyed the kinds of work she'd done in her life—teaching music as a young woman and then keeping house. Work:

Something called that couldn't also be called enjoyment.

Nora said, "Well, it's nice to be here, anyway. What's new?"

Mrs. Barrett lifted her eyes to Heaven. "I don't know where to begin. It's been an awful winter. The Stringers, the Redingtons, the Westhoffs, the Zimmers—everyone's had something." The Stringers, the Redingtons, the Westhoffs, the Zimmers—all summer communities can be broken down into cells; this one took in the boardwalk where the Barretts rented and two or three houses on the next walk. In the life of Mrs. Barrett it was the closest she'd come, since the earliest days of her marriage, to what she might have been in the world where she truly belonged, a small but complete world where everyone knew everyone else and everything about everyone else, though not in a gossipy way; simply as a matter of course. Instead, she and Mr. Barrett had an apartment in the suburbs, and people in apartments tend to guard their privacy. Apartments in the suburbs also have something institutional about them—the way they rise above and miss out on that natural combination of seclusion and sociability that prevails down below. But here at the beach the Barretts came into their own. Mrs. Barrett said, "Paul Redington has lost his job. Sixteen years with that company, and the first thing you know they let him go."

"Isn't that awful."

"They gave up the house in Roslyn and moved in with her people until school closed; then she brought the five children over here."

"What's going to happen now?"

"He's found another job, thank God, but it's in Ohio. He's out there, looking for a place to live, and as soon as he finds something they have to pack up and leave."

Nora's sandals were catching in the cracks between the boards. She stopped to take them off, hopping from one foot to the other as the soles of her feet touched the blazing boardwalk. The trick was to keep to the right; the boards were cooler there, where sprays of shadow fell from the dense shrubbery that lined the walk—beach plums, holly, scrub oak, scrub pine, high enough to spread dark, cool green arches over the crosswalks. Nora was suddenly glad to be there. She hurried and caught up with her mother, who was unaware of having been momentarily on her own and had kept on talking. "Harriet Zimmer's sure he has another woman."

"Mr. Redington?" Nothing could have been more out of the character of that big, amiable man, the ideal father, who spent all day Saturday and Sunday with his two little boys, swimming in the ocean, or out in the bay, clamming and crabbing.

"Not Paul Redington—Joe Rogers. He's hardly ever here on the weekend. Kay Rogers is thin as a rail and a nervous wreck."

"Well, if it's true, I'm not surprised."

Two girls in crocheted bikinis walked by, sipping from cans of beer. Mrs. Barrett looked at them out of the corner of her eye; then, she looked at Nora. Sometimes she wondered about Nora. What did Nora know about life? Surely someone so attractive and intelligent would have learned a thing or two, especially in the advertising world which was known to be very sophisticated. Nora had travelled, too. She'd been to France and Spain and Italy. What had she learned there? What had she done? If Nora had learned nothing, then what was wrong with her? If she'd learned a thing or two, then why hadn't she made those things work for her? Had she made them work against her? How? In the end Mrs. Barrett left all these matters up in the air and fell back on an old theory of hers that there was some flaw in Nora's makeup, something obvious but nevertheless hard to put your finger on. She said, "What do you mean you wouldn't be surprised?"

Nora meant that one evening, when they were having drinks with the Rogerses, Joe had from time to time let out a laugh and slapped his leg and then reached over and squeezed hers, but she said, "I don't know. He just always struck me that way."

"Well, I don't believe there's a word of truth in the story, and I'll tell you why—it seems the Zimmers and the Rogerses don't see eye to eye. Lois Westhoff told me. Poor Lois—she's had a bad time of it, too. Young Bobby ran away right before Christmas. He was heading for California, but luckily the police picked him up in Pennsylvania and brought him home, but he refused to go back to school. Only one more year and he'd be finished with high school and he won't finish the year. I call that a shame."

A little boy and girl were coming along with a wagon, which they now steered in such a way as to keep Nora and her mother from getting past. "Would you like to buy some shells?" the little girl said.

Mrs. Barrett loved children, though she sometimes seemed to love the idea of them better than the real thing. But these two children were ideal. They both had blond hair and freckles; they wore matching striped seersucker sunsuits with a red beetle appliquéd on the pocket; they both looked shy and, at the same time, bold in an enterprising way. She bent down and said, "It all depends on how much you're charging."

"The big ones are a nickel, and the little ones are two for ten cents."

Mrs. Barrett whispered to Nora, "Aren't they the cutest?"

"Adorable." Nora didn't love children, or anyone else, in the aggregate; she loved them in particular, and the children she particularly loved were her sister Joan's four. In a few days, Joan and her husband were bringing the children to spend a week at the beach. They were very real children. They tracked sand into the house. They stayed too long in the shower and left their wet bathing suits on the bathroom floor and forgot about them. They asked not to have too much celery in the tuna-fish sandwiches, and in the middle of the afternoon they got at the breakfast cereal, which they ate dry, spilling it around, drawing ants. They went out too far in the ocean, they wouldn't eat their grandmother's famous baked beans, and after dark they ran down to the club and bought candy bars and ice-cream cones, and they fought. If Nora was there when they were, she spent the time trying to pacify her mother, who ended up either staying at the house all day, keeping track of things, or spending the day on the beach to get away. But all that was nearly a week off.

"Which do you like the best?" Mrs. Barrett held up two shells—one was dead white, the other was discolored; neither was much of a specimen.

"The white, I suppose."

Mrs. Barrett got her change purse from the pocket of her dress. Something in the way she felt through the coins showed she knew the value of nickels and dimes; it also made Nora's heart ache. Her mother was one of ten children, the one who seemed to have regularly got the short end, and also the one her brothers and sisters had apparently made a habit of taking advantage of. There were any number of stories that suggested this, such as the time she'd washed and ironed her brother's shirt for some big event at the last minute, and when she asked him how he liked the job she'd done—wanting a word of praise, poor girl—he said, "Don't think you're indispensable." Mrs. Barrett would tell these stories without a trace of resentment or self-pity. She told them to instruct and to edify, but they sent Nora into a rage that flared up now, as it always would, when she saw her mother being taken in. She said, "I don't know why you're buying shells when you can pick them up for nothing all over the beach."

"Just one." Mrs. Barrett paid her nickel and got her shell. She'd let go of the wagon, and when she reached for the handle again Nora had got hold of it. "Give me that," she protested, but Nora started off, and Mrs. Barrett gave in. She was beginning to be tired, not so much physically as mentally. For days she'd looked forward to seeing Nora, and then Nora came and in a matter of minutes Nora had her worn out. Not that Nora made trouble as such—far from it. She was simply a worry in a way that Joan, on the other hand, never was. Joan told you everything, but with Nora you never knew what was what. It was all very well keeping things to yourself, all very well sparing other people, but in the long run was that good? Was it normal? Where did it get you? Mrs. Barrett said, "Do you remember that brother of Mr. Dinkel's who was up from Mexico with his family the summer before last?"

"Vaguely."

"Well, the oldest girl was married during the winter to a lieutenant commander in the Navy. The wedding was in Washington, D.C., where he was stationed, and they went to Nova Scotia on their honeymoon."

"Ouch!" Nora had got a splinter in her foot. She picked it out and held it up. "First of the year."

"When they got back they went to New London for two months, and then he had orders to join the Sixth Fleet in the Mediterranean. They're there now."

"That's nice." All the grim news had been passed along fairly cheerily, but this happy story sounded a sour note that irritated Nora, even though she was sympathetic. She sincerely wished she could have lived the life her mother wanted her to, but for reasons having almost equally to do with opportunity and choice, her own life had gone in a direction that was bound to be puzzling to Mrs. Barrett. It was a puzzle to Nora herself, in some ways and at some times. When she stayed with Joan and her family, for example, she'd find herself wondering why she, too, wasn't living in a nice house with a big living room, and a cluster of bedrooms, and a sun porch, an attic, a basement, a den, an old-fashioned kitchen, a back yard with trees and flowers and patches of bare ground where the poles that held the badminton net were set up every year. To an extent it was her own fault—Nora would readily admit that. She was uncompromising, but in all decency how could you be otherwise? The nature of anyone's desire, the image of its satisfaction, was the essence of that person. It was the truest thing about you, and not only about you but about the other person as well. It was also the soft spot, the raw spot, the tendency you were born with and that everything that happened to you tended to encourage or to frustrate. You followed it and took your chances, or you went against it and took an even greater chance. In other words, it was nothing to fool around with, and once that actually dawned on you, once it penetrated, either you became cold-blooded or you began to be scrupulous, or maybe it was squeamish, or even timid—or all three. Anyway, you were inclined to draw back from desire that didn't, as desire seldom does, match your own. Her mother, moved by the vaguest of dreams and the greatest common sense, would sometimes put it much more simply. "You're too particular. You think no one's good enough for you." Nora was willing to admit to some truth in this, even though she had no great opinion of herself. If someone had asked her how she thought she appeared to people, her answer would have been something like unobtrusive. And if she'd been asked what she thought was her best quality, she'd have said responsiveness, but lately she'd been less and less prompt with even the simple responses. She disliked listening to herself being herself. She kept hearing things she'd said too many times before, with the result that they no longer seemed to ring quite true. Often she had the feeling of doing an impersonation, and not a good impersonation, and so she began impersonating someone else, someone who was very nice, very agreeable, but incommunicado.

"Incidentally," Mrs. Barrett said, "Helen Munson's brother is down visiting this week."

For some few minutes there'd been the sound of grinding gears and skidding tires behind them, a vehicle moving in fits and starts, sticking in the sand and then heaving forward with the maximum pitch and roll possible in the narrow track beside the boardwalk. Mrs. Barrett turned around. A truck was slowly gaining on them. "It's Sam Tucker," she said.

The Tuckers were Mrs. Barrett's model family, the epitome of all she'd ever wanted in her own family. To begin with, Sam owned a good slice of this part of the island—at least a dozen of the most comfortable houses, one of which the Barretts had rented for a couple of seasons. He was a tall man with wavy gray hair, and he always had a captain's hat pushed back on his head. During the week, he wore a bathing suit day and night, but on the weekend he sometimes broke out in colored silk shirts with immaculate white linen or duck trousers. The Tuckers spent most of the year in Florida and the rest of their time here, in a house that faced the bay and was situated so as to make the sunset appear to be something arranged on their behalf—arranged by Sam. Having done away with winter, Molly Tucker was always tan, and, having the willpower and Sam to spur her on, she was also always thin, and she dressed in colors that Sam picked out—turquoise, lime, gold, orange. Whereas, at the beach Mrs. Barrett wore shoes that laced and, because she was susceptible to chills, a pair of white cotton socks. And though her clothes were always in good taste, good taste and high style aren't necessarily the same. As for Mr. Barrett, when he was living the rugged life he threw any old thing on him; the older his outfit the better he felt. That these weren't superficial aspects of life, that they could define and separate people, was something Mrs. Barrett didn't understand. She looked across the gulf and saw only that she wanted to be and for some reason wasn't close to the Tuckers. Arms reached out the windows of the red truck and waved, voices shouted hello, but the truck passed by.

Mrs. Barrett said, "Wait till you see him. He's a knockout."

"Who?"

"Helen Munson's brother. He's a district attorney up in Connecticut. That reminds me," she went on, knowing (though she didn't always act on the knowledge) that there was such a thing as going too far, and also wanting to pass along another bit of news she'd been reminded of—the Munsons lived next door to the Sayres, and the Sayres hadn't been spared in the past winter—"Jane Sayre lost her father last March."

Nora couldn't resist. She said, "Did they look everywhere?" There was just so much you could take of other people's troubles.

"Jane Sayre was devoted to her father and he to her. Ever since she was married, he used to drive up to visit them once a month. He never missed a month the whole time. I think that's something."

The last crosswalk was a few feet ahead. Nora steered the wagon around the corner and up a short grade, turned in at the first deck on the right, and brought the wagon around to the door at the side of the house. Once she stopped moving, the heat hit her.

Mrs. Barrett said, "Would you like a glass of iced tea?"

"I'd love it."

"Sit there and I'll bring it out to you."

"Don't bother, I'll get it," said Nora. "I want to take my stuff inside."

The house was taller than most beach cottages, and on account of that it seemed marvellously bright and roomy, though it was hardly more than this one big room, presided over by a black wood-burning stove, which was decidedly off-center, dividing the room unevenly. To the left were matching bamboo chairs and sofa. There were also a couple of yellow canvas chairs, a couple of wooden stools, a low table, and a bookcase with—Nora saw at a glance—some new paperbacks since the summer before. To the right of the stove there was nothing but a wide daybed, piled with cushions—a wonderful spot to stretch out and read on a rainy day. The kitchen was behind a counter, near the door. Mrs. Barrett got a jar of tea from the refrigerator. "Lemon?" she said.

"No thanks." Nora dropped her bags and went and sat down facing the wall that was one huge window. Her objections to being waited on had evaporated. She was more than grateful for the glass of tea her mother brought over—she found the sight of it chastening. Too much love is a burden, but the existence of that love, its modesty and its endurance, can sometimes be heartening and even its most obtuse demonstrations touching. Nora smiled at the slice of lemon stuck on the glass.

"That's for decoration."

Nora took it off and put it on the plate and had a long drink. "Heavenly," she said. "Just what I feel like. Thank you."

Mrs. Barrett sat down in one of the canvas chairs and folded her hands across her stomach. "Well, I've given you all my news," she said, "now tell me what's new with you."

"I got a raise."

Mrs. Barrett nodded in a way that implied consent, the vote of approval that made things official. "I'm very glad to hear that," she said. Also implicit in her nod and in her voice was the sum of her experience with the world, which amounted to the fact that recognition was hard to come by. Mr. Barrett, a man of fine intelligence, had never received the slightest recognition. On the other hand, a young woman wrapped up in her job was a young woman who ran the risk of finding herself wrapped up in it for good. "Heaven knows you deserve a break. I've never seen anyone work so hard, and what have you got to show for it?"

"At the minute I have a little headache. That train ride was brutal." Nora took another long drink of tea and then leaned her head back, gazing out the big window. Across the walk was the pale-green cottage her parents had rented from the Tuckers until young Carol Tucker got married and had a baby; after that, Carol and Jack and their little girl Janet used the house. Now the door banged open and Janet came bursting out.

Mrs. Barrett said, "Do you by any chance remember those people who visited the Tuckers last year?"

"Which people?" The Tuckers were always having people for the weekend—big prosperous-looking men like Sam; trim, smiling women like Molly.

"A couple slightly on in years—he worked for Sam. She'd been a nurse, and they married late in life. She was about forty-three or four, and he was five or six years older. They had a little boy named Andrew."

Nora remembered in an instant and with a gust of feeling that took her by surprise. "Yes," she said.

"He was the dearest little fellow."

"I remember." Two and a half or three years old, with thick, short, straight, dark-blond hair; fat little arms, fat little legs; a stocky body in a bright-red woolen bathing suit with a navy-blue waistband.

"I think the Tuckers had the family over as a kind of favor. I believe the father had done some extra work for Sam. He was the manager of Sam's place, I believe Carol said. Carol was very nice to them, and the little boy and Janet had a good time together. He was a real little boy."

Out on the walk, Janet was riding her tricycle, pedalling up a grade and then lifting her feet and skimming back down. She was four this year, and her play had an industrious look about it, but last summer she'd been a tempermental playmate, though the little boy, little Andrew, had unintentionally—in fact, with the best will in the world—thwarted all her efforts to rile him. She threw sand at him and he laughed. She stole his shovel and he presented her with the bucket, too. She splashed him in the water and he ran around in circles, merrily splashing himself. Andrew. It was a down-to-earth name, but it also had a distinguished sound that suggested a whole order of rare and wonderful qualities —loyalty, honor, insight, candor, courage, grace, strength of character, depth of feeling, breadth of understanding, goodness of heart; qualities this Andrew had given the impression of being ready someday to live up to, even to extend beyond their ordinary meanings. Nora also got the impression, unfounded but nevertheless very definite, that the name had been chosen with no one else in mind, that it hadn't come from his father or a grandfather or some uncle or friend of the family, that it was his exclusively. Andrew—he was the embodiment of his beautiful name.

"Well," said Mrs. Barrett, "it seems during the winter little Andrew developed a growth on his toe. He was operated on, and the doctor found out it was cancerous. It spread through his entire body and in six months he was dead. Carol said the mother nearly lost her mind. She can't have any more children—I suppose on account of her age —and Andrew was all they had. According to Carol, the mother wanted her husband to get a divorce so that he at least could have a family, but naturally he wouldn't. He said there'd never be another Andrew anyway, and they don't want to adopt, either, for the same reason. They both adored that child. He was their whole world and yet he wasn't the least bit spoiled, he was as good as gold. The disposition of him, why—" Mrs. Barrett stopped short. Nora was starting to cry like a baby. Wasn't that the limit! Of all the tragedy there was in life, of all the tragedies that had struck over the past winter, grave things that, only minutes before, Nora had been ready to dismiss—after all that, who could have thought this thing would have such an effect on Nora, Nora who never even paid that much attention to children. "He was one of the Holy Innocents. That's the way to look at it. God wanted him for Himself. The Lord gives and the Lord takes away." Mrs. Barrett handed Nora a Kleenex. "That's brand-clean," she said. "It's only crushed from being in my pocket." Nora blew her nose, but she didn't seem to be making the slightest effort to stop crying. Mrs. Barrett became a little concerned. "He took a shine to you that afternoon. I remember now."

"He didn't take a shine to me. I just played with him for a minute."

"Yes, towards the end of the day. They stayed on the beach till late, to get the most out of it, because they were only here the one day. But it was a glorious day."

A clear, cloudless blue day right up until late afternoon, when the sky began giving pinkish intimations of the sunset to come. Nora had stayed on the beach to keep her mother company, and her mother was staying there until all her grandchildren were sure to be finished with the shower. Nora remembered having a book with her—a mystery, a Simenon. She also remembered having been not very good company, but it didn't matter, because her mother struck up a conversation with the woman who was visiting the Tuckers —a nice woman with a bemused air, the entranced and vulnerable look of someone whose dream has come true. The little boy was playing by himself. Finally, Nora had enough of the beach. She put down her book and sat for a minute looking out at the water—so mild-mannered that afternoon, like a gentle, introspective friend, someone who doesn't necessarily prefer talk to silence. Lying nearby on the sand was the dismembered beach umbrella—the green-and-yellow striped canvas top and the pointed lower half of the pole. In his solitary play, the little boy hit on the pole and, seeing her idle for a minute, offered it to her. She stuck it firmly in the sand and said, "There."

His blue eyes lit up, with enthusiasm, with satisfaction at discovering he'd done the right thing, and with a powerful longing to keep on doing it. He lifted the pole out of the sand, planted it himself, and announced, "There!" Nora clapped, and he pulled up the pole and replanted it. "There!" he cried again, and Nora clapped again. They played this game seven or eight times. The little boy, of course, could have gone on indefinitely, and maybe earlier in the day Nora would have lasted a little longer or eased her way out more gently, but it was late, and she was ready to leave the beach. There was sand inside her bathing suit, and her skin was flaked from the salt water; her hair was a mess. She wanted to have a shower and get into clean clothes. She got up and folded her beach chair. The little boy stared—he'd just planted the pole. Nora said, "Goodbye, Andrew."

His sorrow, like his happiness, was sweet and manly. The light simply left his blue eyes; his little mouth made an attempt at some question, but he made no sound. You'd have said he was responding the way he always would—with his whole heart, with no reservations and no pretense and yet without excess. Nora's reaction was also true to her. With a thorough sense of failure and self-reproach and self-dislike, all of it disguised, she picked up her chair and the canvas part of the umbrella. She remembered thinking that her mother would bring up the pole and that he could play with it till then. "Goodbye, Andrew," she repeated and began to back away. He stood perfectly still, his hand on the pole, a small sentry, guarding the gray sea and the deserted beach. She waved, but he didn't move. She waved again and smiled and started across the sand. Every so often she turned and waved, and every time she did she found him standing there stock still, his hand on the pole, his fat little legs up to the ankles in sand, his red swimming trunks bright and sad, the emblem of a lost cause. At the top of the steps to the boardwalk, she turned and waved one last time; then she went back to the house and had her shower and washed her hair, and her father made her a gin-and-tonic, and she agreed to a game of cards with two of her nieces.

Mrs. Barrett said, "He did too take a shine to you. After you left the beach that day, he went over to his mother and said, 'Girl gone,' and then he laid his head in her lap and stayed that way till they left the beach." Nora tried to blow her nose again, but the Kleenex was all used up; she threw it at the table and shot up off the sofa—it was very strange behavior, and Mrs. Barrett began to be more than a little concerned. She wondered, as she sometimes felt she must, whether Nora was a little unbalanced. Or was it a question of nutrition? Should Nora be taking vitamins? Mrs. Barrett was on the verge of tears herself when the side door opened —Mr. Barrett was back from the beach.

Like his wife, though in different ways, Francis Barrett gave the impression that the course of his life had been far smoother than was actually the case. He was wiry, only partially gray, had a chipper air and an amused expression, and at the moment was dripping wet. He shook himself all over like a dog and said, "Greetings. How was the trip?"

"Awful," Mrs. Barrett answered for Nora, though Nora had suddenly calmed down and could have answered for herself. That was her way—completely unpredictable.

Something or other came along and you'd think it was the end of the world; then, another time, tell her something just as terrible, or worse, and she'd only shrug. Mrs. Barrett herself gave an inward shrug—a just perceptible shudder. The line of thought she'd been following was familiar to her, and it led always to the same scene, her deathbed. She saw it as a time of listlessness and confusion, with people standing around at loose ends; then she saw herself dead, lying in state in the corner of a strange room, cold and silent, while life and talk went on all around her; then she saw herself being buried—shoved into the ground, left there and forgotten.

Nora said, "How was the ocean?"

"Like a lake," said Mr. Barrett. "If I were you I'd get into my suit and get down there and have a dip."

"Maybe I will," Nora said, but she made no move in that direction or any other, till her mother called to her.

"Look, Nora!" Mrs. Barrett could be every bit as changeable as Nora. She could also be much more easily distracted —having greater faith and therefore stronger bonds with everything around her—and momentarily, but for that moment completely, she now forgot her worries. "Quickly, out on the walk," she said.

Nora turned and saw a man in uniform riding by on a beautiful chestnut horse, sedately pacing the animal in the sand track beside the boardwalk.

Mrs. Barrett said, "That's one of the forest rangers. They're all over the place, now that the island's a national park. Just wait till you see the difference it's made on the beach. The dunes have been built up, the tide line's been built up, everything's improved."

The horse and rider passed out of sight, but Nora kept on looking out the window. An old woman was going by now, an old woman in black, just like the woman on the boat, except that this one had no cakebox. Instead, she was carrying a mop and a pail and a shopping bag that looked as if it were stuffed with dusters. Nora said, "Who's that?"

"One of the cleaning ladies," Mrs. Barrett said. "They're another new thing this year. A group of old women from the mainland got together and organized themselves, and they come and do housekeeping. I understand they charge an arm and a leg."

The bedrooms in the cottage were tiny, with a strong cedar smell and no furniture except bunk beds and built-in closets. Nora used a room at the back that was surrounded by bushes, but it was a spot that didn't get much light and so the branches were thin, and from the window you could see a stretch of deck that was the entrance to the cottage. She put her suitcase on the floor and got out her bathing suit and was unzipping her dress when she heard a truck rumble to a stop nearby. A man began giving orders. There was a sound of something being unloaded. It was too late in the day for the garbage collectors, and Sam Tucker was already home from the mainland; it was either the plumber, builders, or the gasman. Nora waited. After a minute or two, a boy carrying a tank of gas appeared on the walk and turned in at their deck. Behind him came Mr. Ascappo, who sold bottled gas and was in charge of the waterworks.

It was always a shock, always uncanny, and, no matter how often you came on him, never the least bit less shocking or less uncanny to see the resemblance between the gasman and Picasso. They might have been twins—identical twins, with the same short, tough, square body; the same blazing black eyes that could suddenly show that look of clever clownishness; the same big nose; the same sparse fringe of white hair, curving over the ears and around the base of the skull. Even their way of dressing was the same, though old men in hot sunny places often appear in baggy shorts and a loose jersey. Common or not, Mr. Ascappo's clothes car-

ried out the likeness. Then there was the name, Ascappo—
almost an anagram of the painter's name.

The boy lowered the tank of gas to the deck and jumped
down to the sand. Mr. Ascappo eased the tank into the boy's
arms and then placed his own hands on his hips. It was the
fierce standing crouch that had confronted canvas and
brought off "La Femme Fleur," "Les Saltimbanques," "Les
Demoiselles d'Avignon," "Guernica." "Steady," said Mr.
Ascappo, and the remarkable effect was slightly spoiled. The
indifferent voice and the careless movement of the wide, flat
lips were out of keeping, but then again, thought Nora,
maybe that was a failure of her own imagination. For the
painter's phenomenal zest must surely have deserted him
from time to time. Waking in the night, wondering where
he was, thirsty, wanting to know the time or to go to the
bathroom, even he would have had to briefly bear witness
to the underlying meagreness of life, as Mr. Ascappo did
every time he opened his mouth. But in any case the illusion
was hardly ever spoiled. The gasman was taciturn. He made
his rounds, delivering his tanks of propane in practically
unbroken silence; in silence he could be seen wandering
behind the barbed-wire fence that marked off his other
territory—the generator and the big blue drum of the waterworks.

The boy removed the empty gas tank and installed the full
one—a simple operation. Mr. Ascappo gave him a hand
back up onto the deck; they walked off and out of sight;
another minute and the truck started up, and they drove
away. Nora finished unzipping her dress and took it off; she
loosened her hair and picked up her bathing suit, and then
she put it down again and went over and stretched out on
the lower bunk and folded her arms across her face. She
thought of the old woman in the black dress. Or was it the
old women? Were there two—one with a cakebox, having
an outing; one with a mop, going to work—or were they the

same? She thought of Picasso, of the magnificently cluttered rooms where he'd often been pictured, and of the stupefying inventiveness and proliferation of his work. She thought of the Madonna, rapt and oblivious, against a prospect of some distant Flemish, or Spanish, or Italian village. She thought of the stately horseback rider in his ranger's uniform and his cap like a Canadian Mountie's. She thought of Mr. Ascappo. All these images were provocative, all disturbing, and in somewhat the same way. Resemblances, contrasts, contradictions, coincidence, anomaly, incongruity, ambiguity— the spirit that moves the world has these wonderful resources with which to confound us. We live at the mercy of that spirit, and the spirit lets us live, by and large, in ignorance, and lest you lose sight of it, from time to time you receive some exceptional reminder of your ignorance. Take Mr. Ascappo. He was like the brilliant afterthought, the deliberate clue that the legendary criminal genius leaves behind, the touch that can belong to him and no other. He knows, and everyone knows, that the difficulty will lie not in putting the finger on him but in capturing him, and so, instead of having to cover the traces, he can indulge himself, add some inimitable flourish. Nora saw him, this casual virtuoso, far from the scene of the crime, picturing that scene, sorry to be no longer a part of it, imagining what short work he himself would have made of the investigation: Something of infinite value is gone. Who's responsible? Who else! But should there be any doubts, let me call attention to something, a small thing and irrelevant to the case except that it shows what you're up against. This Mr. Ascappo, the gasman, who looks like Picasso. Yes, he's a familiar figure around here, but don't be fooled, look closely, see him now for what he is—the signature of the master.

Only Human

It was a terrible, terrible shock. The night before, I was
talking to him on the telephone, and he said he was fine but,
of course, he wouldn't have let on. He was forever thinking
of others, never of himself, and that was how he spent his
last day on earth, thinking of others." This line was the
climax of Mrs. Cunningham's story of the death of her
brother, Father James Murray, the Jesuit, but telling the
story now to a group of nuns at the wake she'd somehow let
the line slip into the very beginning. She had to stop and
collect her thoughts, and the nuns took her to be overcome
with feeling. Two of them were nursing sisters in traditional
long white habits; the four others wore drab black dresses,
improvised habits that were each slightly different but
looked all alike, not so much habits as the uniform of the
new Church.

"There never was a superior like Father Jim Murray," one
of the nursing sisters said. Apart from the family, the nuns
were the only people at the wake just then, but half a dozen
of them plus the half dozen or so Murrays gave an impression of twice that number, because the room was so small

and so ornate, like a miniature ballroom. It was a reception parlor there at the university, where Father Murray had spent most of his twenty-odd years as a priest and where, for the last two years, he'd been an assistant superior. "Whenever any of his men were at the hospital," the nursing sister went on, "we never had to worry about their being lonely or neglected, because we knew Father Murray would look after them, whether they had family or not and whether or not the family was attentive. He gave of himself unstintingly."

"Unstintingly," Mrs. Cunningham agreed, "right to the very end." She was a good-hearted woman, well over sixty but still pretty, and with a motherly look, but her natural warmth and attractiveness were spoiled by the way she was throwing herself into all the sad details of this sad story. She couldn't help herself, though. She'd never felt that she was as close to her brother as she would have liked, as close, as a matter of fact, as she felt now. She was making up for lost time. "That Tuesday was the first anniversary of the death of Father Bill Kearns, Dolly and Rita Kearns's brother, and they wanted Father Jim to say the anniversary Mass, so he had to travel all the way out to Brooklyn. Afterward, he went along to the cemetery; then the Kearns girls insisted he go back to their place for lunch, and he did; he went and had a meat-loaf sandwich and from there he went to the hospital where Father Steve Cusack is in with ulcers. By the time he finally got home his hip must have been bothering him terribly."

"Had the hip been broken?" asked a thin, very plain but very sweet-looking nun.

"No, Sister, he had arthritis in his whole lower left side. Walking aggravated it, and I'm sure he was in great pain when I talked to him, but all he said was he thought he'd go to bed early. During the night Brother Desnoes, who had the room next door, heard moaning, but he figured Father's hip was acting up, so he thought no more about it. Six o'clock next morning, Father Jim got the nurse on the phone, and they rushed him to Mercy Hospital. I had a call from Father Minister at half past eleven and I asked him if I should come, but he said, 'There's no immediate danger, Mrs. Cunningham.'" Her imitation of a sharp, clipped voice suggested a grudge being harbored, if not cherished. *(If I'd paid attention to that Father Davis, and thanks be to God I didn't . . .)* "All the same I felt I should make the effort, but I couldn't reach Mr. Cunningham and I was afraid of the delay on the bus, and there was no use calling Marjorie." She glanced at the young woman sitting over by the door, and again her voice had an edge to it, but this time there was a simple explanation—the fact that her daughter, Marjorie, was sitting alone when she could have been with her Uncle Bob, the bachelor, and her aunt, Sister Grace Marie, or with her Uncle Joe, who was a colonel in the Army and had come up from Virginia with his wife, Sally, and their two teen-age boys; or she could have been with her father. To Mrs. Cunningham, Marjorie's solitariness made her look as if she'd walked in off the street, but only to Mrs. Cunningham, because Marjorie's clothes—her plain black dress, her black patent shoes, and her heavy white sweater —showed a real regard for the occasion. Her dark blond hair was held back by a narrow black velvet band. She wore face powder and lipstick and no other makeup, and no jewelry. She was someone who would always look the way she was supposed to look, someone who had a horror of standing out, though she did like being by herself. Mrs. Cunningham said, "Marjorie has no car. She hasn't the need for one, living down there in the city."

"What did you do?" the thin nun murmured, sensing trouble and wanting to smooth it over.

"I called a young friend of ours, a girl who went to school with my older daughter, Caroline. We were at the hospital in twenty minutes, and as soon as I walked into the room I thanked God I'd come. There was death in his face."

"And this was from his hip?"

"No, Sister, an infection of the pancreas. He'd just been put in an oxygen tent when I got there, and I went over to him and said, 'Jim, dear, it's Helen,' and he went"—she bobbed her head—"and his mouth moved"—she gagged realistically—"as if he wanted me to know he knew I was there, so I began to talk to him. 'You're the best brother anyone could ever want,' I said. 'I love you dearly, but you have to be quiet now and get better. Let everybody take care of you for a change instead of you taking care of everybody else. Because,' I said, 'you're the most generous, most loving fellow in the whole world, and we can't let anything happen to you, but you have to help, you have to relax.' "

"He wasn't conscious then, was he?" one of the nursing nuns quietly suggested.

"I think he must have been just going," Mrs. Cunningham said, "but I never stopped talking to him from the time I got there, which was a quarter past twelve, till almost the very end."

Small as it was, the room where the wake was being held had two big windows and two big doors. The windows were each open a crack, the doors were both wide open, and the place was freezing. This was the second coldest January 10th on record; a few days earlier there'd been a blizzard, and off and on since then there'd been snow showers. The university grounds looked beautiful, but the old fieldstone buildings like this one, the lovely old Administration Building, were hard to heat. Marjorie Cunningham (who'd been Marjorie Peck for three years) wrapped her sweater more closely around her. It was five o'clock, the slow time of the wake. Not enough people were there in the room to block the drafts, but any minute now Father Davis would come and take the family to dinner in the priests' dining room, over in the priests' residence, a new building, where it would be warm. It was strange to Marjorie, going inside there—four or five years before, women hadn't been allowed in the buildings where the priests lived, and men who weren't priests could only go as far as the front hall. Four or five years ago, she herself would probably not even have been on this campus. She'd been married to a man who was divorced, but now she was divorced from him—divorced for a year, married for three. She tilted her head back and concentrated on a curlicue of the molding near the high ceiling of the little room. All that happiness and all that misery—there was very little to choose between them, she thought. Good luck and bad luck amounted to pretty much the same thing in the end, except that the good was more trouble. It was harder to live with happiness because you couldn't forget about it. You were too full of it—you were blown up by it. But unhappiness brought you down to size. All you wanted was to get it out of your mind and you did. So in that sense she could honestly say it was pretty much the same to her now which way things went for her. What happened to other people was more interesting. She thought of what had happened to Father Jim, but thinking of him, she was forced to think of herself, too, for strangely enough her life and his had clashed, six years before, when she'd met Harry Peck, and Father Jim was rector here at the university—not an especially popular rector. There'd been factions in the community, and the breath of scandal had been one more strike against him, one among a lot of other strikes, for the wheels of change were just then beginning to turn, and he'd been of the old school, not quite ready for the change and not quite able to stand up to it or back from it. But now the Church itself had had a real dose of scandal. Defections, heresy, a generalized discontent and disorder in the ranks— all that gave Marjorie the sense of having been ahead of the times, which, it turned out, was the last thing in the world she'd wanted. What had she wanted?

"Marjorie!"

She'd wanted to lose her way and then find it again, find it for herself, if the way was there and could be found. But while her back was turned a trick had been played on her; everything was switched around. She got up and went over to her mother and the group of nuns.

"Marjorie is my younger daughter," Mrs. Cunningham said. "My older girl, Caroline, and her husband, Frank, will be here tonight. They live in Boston with their four children, two boys and two girls."

"The perfect family," said a tiny nun, bright as a bird. "And what do you do, Marjorie?"

I don't do anything. I'm divorced. That was the truth, as good an answer as any, but not the right answer for this nice, enthusiastic little nun. Marjorie thought of the job she'd once had and would probably have again one of these days, when she had to do something. "I'm a proofreader," she said.

"My, that must be interesting!"

"It's not really," Marjorie said. "It's very exacting, like sewing."

"There's something I'd love to be able to do—sew. Sister Renata here is an expert. She made nearly all these new habits of ours—I say made but I really mean remade. We got the dresses, castoffs, from our families, and Sister altered them to fit us and then made the white collars and cuffs and the headpieces. She can make suits, blouses—she even made a coat once, but she says she won't tackle *that* job again in a hurry!"

In the old days, nuns had been all sacrifice. They'd given up everything, given it up for you (and let you know it), but then they discovered themselves. They blossomed out. You saw them in department stores or in the five-and-ten, buying stockings and hair spray, looking, on the whole, a little pathetic. What a bad bargain they'd made—giving up the sense of mystery for this new but hopelessly dated clothes sense. Marjorie said, "Do you ever miss the old habits, Sister?"

"I should say not! As your dear uncle, Father Murray, used to say, we like being in the swim. He was a terrible tease, wasn't he?"

"He was." And in ways this nice nun wouldn't have come up against.

"But he had tremendous warmth, too."

"He did." Always taking you aside and telling you, in that beautiful, cultivated voice, some dirty joke; always, when he kissed you, touching you some place he shouldn't have touched you; always those wet kisses.

"And patience! I never, in all the years I knew him, ever saw him lose his temper!"

Neither did I, it occurred to Marjorie. "The most generous, most loving fellow in the whole world"—there was some truth in that description of her mother's, but there was a lot more to the truth, a lot more to the man. He'd been terribly complicated, not someone you'd have thought of as a priest. Maybe being a priest had created the complications, exaggerated all those feelings he was supposed to have given up, though they hadn't given him up, had never, probably, given him a moment's real peace. If he'd got married maybe he wouldn't have been so at the mercy of his feelings or been so generous and loving. He might have drawn back the way people did, retreating to some position there was at least a hope of holding.

"Will you excuse me, Marjorie?" the nun asked. "I see Father John Zimmerman." A priest with an overcoat over his cassock had just come into the room, along with a man in a tan duffel coat. "I must go and say hello," the nun said. It was the man in the duffel coat she went and spoke to.

Marjorie looked over at the figure that had become for her the one sure point of reference in the room, Brother Desnoes, the lay brother. For the last three days he'd stood in that same corner, his hands in his pockets or tucked under his arms, or one hand touching the end of the long side table, his close-set, brown, shoe-button eyes staring into the crowd or over all the heads, a rough, healthy peasant out of Flaubert. Why would a man, especially a man like that, become a brother? It was a nondescript life, the so-called "lay" side of a religious order. If this man hadn't joined up, what would he have been? A waiter, maybe. A very good waiter in a very good restaurant. He had the serious confidence of someone who knows his job and enjoys showing he can do it perfectly. Marjorie saw him in a tuxedo, taking orders, serving plates—*the Chateaubriand? the veal scaloppine?*—keeping his mind on his work, saying almost nothing. It struck her then that she hadn't noticed anyone talking with Brother Desnoes during the wake, any of the family. She was thinking of going over and starting up a conversation when someone took her by the arm.

"Is anybody hungry?"

It was Father Davis, come to collect them.

The dining hall was huge, and on two sides it consisted of floor-to-ceiling windows that were uncurtained, turned into mirrors by the black winter evening, so that they gave back two more vast, bare, brilliantly lit, depressing rooms with the general effect of a cafeteria rather than anything more spiritually refined that the word "refectory" might suggest.

The place was empty when Father Murray's family arrived. They could have fit at one table (these few surviving members of a family of nine) but they split up because priests from the community had been joining them each evening, as a gesture of hospitality. Mr. and Mrs. Cunningham, Sister Grace Marie, and Bob Murray sat down to-

gether. Joe and Sally went with Marjorie and the two boys
to another table.

"*Komban wa,*" Joe Murray, who'd been stationed in
Tokyo, greeted the Japanese waiter.

The little man grinned and bowed. "*Komban wa,* Colonel," he said.

"*Ikaga desuka?*"

"*Genki desu,* Colonel, *genki desu.*"

Sally Murray had a pleasant look on her face, but she
seemed to have started concentrating on something else.
The boys looked embarrassed; Majorie looked amused; but
Joe, who was not so much gregarious as overenergetic, kept
on talking Japanese until the Jesuits began coming into the
dining room; then he stopped and set himself to seeing
which priests he recognized. Men of all ages breezed
through the swinging doors, but something about them all
—and not their black clothes—seemed to give them a kind
of common age; it could be said of the young men that there
was something old about them, and of the old that they had
an air of youthfulness, or, at least, youngness. One other
thing was true of the group as a whole—they were all in a
hurry. Even the very aged who hobbled in with canes or on
crutches looked as if they had only a little time to put in
here. But what was there for them to do afterward? Sit
around in the lounge next door? And if the refectory was like
a cafeteria, the lounge was like the waiting room in a railroad
station.

As the priests passed the family tables, most of them
nodded. Some waved. And those who knew the Murrays
well came over and said a few words. But the two who took
the pair of empty places between Marjorie and Joe had to
introduce themselves. Joe said, "I can't get over the generosity of you Jesuits, having us share your meal like this."

"It's to show our enormous regard for your brother," said
the priest whose name was Morris. He was a small man with

gray hair parted in the center over the face of a saint—a scholar-saint. A scholar-saint with a sense of humor.

Marjorie said, "I wonder if it's a good idea."

"It's an excellent idea," Joe cut her off—in his opinion Marjorie should have been cut off altogether; he couldn't see that she was anything but a troublemaker, a proven troublemaker. "We'd be at least an hour at a restaurant," he said, "by the time we ordered and were served and had our dinner. To say nothing of the inconvenience."

The other priest, the one right next to Marjorie, who hadn't caught his name, turned to her and asked, "Why do you disapprove?"

"I was half joking," she said. And half serious. "But it does seem to me that opening up something that's always been closed can be unsettling."

"I think we clergy can afford to be a little unsettled," he said. He was a handsome man with a nervous, excitable manner that gave him the look, though he was tall and fairly well built, of being worn down, worn away from what he was meant to be, possibly a bit chipped as well. "I think it may even be good for us. We've had things very easy for a very long time."

"I didn't mean unsettling for you, Father."

He laughed. He had bad, very small, widely spaced teeth. "Do you mean to say you can't take being unsettled?"

"I guess not," Marjorie said. "Not gracefully, anyway."

He laughed again. "Which of the Cunningham girls are you?"

"Marjorie," she said, "the younger one." The one who caused the trouble. Something told her he knew that very well—something alert and knowing in his eyes and in his voice. She changed the subject. "Do you teach, Father?"

"I do indeed, I teach theology. If you can say that theology can be taught, and of course it can't. I'm giving it up next semester."

Nuns had become clothes-conscious, priests had become independent-minded. Marjorie looked around the table for help, but Sally had got into a conversation with Father Morris—across Joe, who was busy taking serving dishes from the Japanese waiter; the boys had their eyes on the food.

"You don't teach God," said the priest. "You have to know Him and you don't get to know Him from a course in a university."

Marjorie said, "Any place is good for a start, isn't it?"

"Not at all, and a classroom is the worst place in the world. God is people and their relationships to each other and to Him. Think, for example, of your uncle."

She thought, again, of her uncle and herself, of the old scandal and the trouble it had caused among men like this man and like the others at the nearby tables. The room was half full now. In the clash of a hundred forks against a hundred plates, in the drone of all that routine conversation there was the sense of mortal dreariness, of day-to-dayness so devoid of the play of deep feelings as to make any man, you'd have thought, desperate. Communal life. The priest-hood. There was more to it than stalls in a chapel, Divine Office being chanted, more to it than prayers and holiness and self-sacrifice. There was this other side that was really institutional life—men at loose ends, each one thrown back on himself because there was no one other person who really knew what he was like; no one who was involved in what happened to him; no one particularly wanting to please him. Take the simplest things, like meals—like this food being handed around the table now: a platter of overdone lamb chops, dishes of vegetables ready too early and kept warming in the kitchen too long. She helped herself to the dried-out broccoli. Imagine that kind of thing night after night. Imagine sitting down night after night with what really must amount to a crowd of acquaintances and having to be pleasant (or unpleasant), making conversation, probably passing on bits of gossip. Yes, of course, there'd be gossip—it was all too plain; they were only human, like Father Jim. Marjorie said, "My uncle was a terribly kind man, terribly forgiving." It sounded like the same old line that had been handed out all during the wake. *He was the soul of kindness. He gave of himself unstintingly. He lived for others.* "But he was terribly vulnerable," she added.

"In what way?"

She'd meant to say something that would give the dead man back a little of what had made him alive, but she'd said the wrong thing. She tried to explain. "It was so important to him to be close to people."

"The impression he gave around here was just the opposite. Some of us used to feel he was inclined to put on airs and throw his weight around."

Marjorie said, "That's something different from what I had in mind."

"What was that?"

The dirty jokes, the wet kisses, the touching. It was easy enough to see what all that came down to, what the truth about anyone could be traced to. "His family," she said. "There were a lot of children, and he was in the middle. And their mother was the classic matriarch." Probably half the men in the room had the same or a very similar story; probably this man did, too. Yes, definitely. Marjorie could tell by the way he was frowning over his plate that she'd hit home. She was prepared for a new offensive, but he surprised her.

He said, "Oddly enough, in these last couple of years the people who hadn't got along with Father Murray before were the very ones who admired him. He changed, you know. He grew mellow with time and with the events of the times even though he had no real desire for changes in the Church. But that made it even more praiseworthy that he was able to overcome his prejudices."

It was almost an about-face. It put Marjorie to shame and made her resent this man who'd been drawing her out for reasons that were not quite clear but were clearly not simple friendliness. She said, "Who ever does want something to be drastically changed when it's a thing you care about?"

"Don't tell me you're a conservative."

"I'm not an anything," she said. "I just miss the old indifference of the Church."

"Because it let *you* be indifferent."

"Because it was like the indifference of God. Would you pass me the butter, Father?" It was a silly, obvious sort of rudeness, and the priest didn't take offense. "What do you do, Marjorie?" he asked politely as he handed her the dish.

"I don't do anything, I'm divorced." This time she succeeded in embarrassing him, not so much by what she said (which he very probably already did know) but because she'd given a loaded answer to a simple question. She'd embarrassed herself, too—more so when she realized that saintly, scholarly Father Morris had overheard her. Their eyes met, and she found herself facing the old, stern sorrow, the kind disapproval, all that was tough, true, really impossible, and necessary—the Church.

These evenings had to end early and so they also had to begin early. By half past six, when the Murray family returned to the Administration Building, visitors were already waiting patiently in the drafty little room—some old friends, some nuns, a couple of elderly women of the retired office-worker type that priests will befriend or be befriended by in the course of a life of needing and dispensing small favors. The hours ahead looked like a grim prospect. Why should she stick it out, Marjorie wondered. Because it hadn't been asked or apparently even expected of her. Because it was the least she could do. Because the one real reason for leaving —that she felt like it—seemed to her just as much a reason for staying. She hung up her coat and turned to the room. Brother Desnoes was back at his corner post, the picture of simple faith, simple devotion. She went over to him and put out her hand. "You're awfully good to have been here all along, Brother," she said.

He took the hand and quickly let it drop again. There was no change of expression in his shoe-button eyes. "I'm in charge," he said.

"Well, you've been wonderful," Marjorie said, hugging her sweater around her self-consciously.

"Are you cold?" he asked.

"A little."

He shook his head. "I don't know what I can do about it."

"That's all right, Brother."

"We have to keep these windows open a crack, don't you know."

"I understand," Marjorie said, but it turned out she didn't.

"Otherwise the hot air might ruin him—even in winter. You can never really tell. Some of them hold up three days, four days, others start going black the first day."

She wondered if she was hearing right.

"And with all the people kissing them the face gets spoiled and I have to fix it up."

She was hearing right. "*You* have to?"

"The undertaker charges about a hundred dollars for a touch-up, but I do it and they pay me twenty-five or thirty dollars. I give it to my sister."

This was the trouble with vague, kindly impulses. You never knew what you were letting yourself in for and more often than not you got stuck, unless you had the courage to run away, and Marjorie didn't. She resigned herself to keeping up the conversation. "Do you come from a large family, Brother?"

"No, just myself and the two sisters—one of them's dead now. We buried her last year."

"I'm awfully sorry."

"She was the younger sister, two years younger than me."

"Had she been very sick?"

"She had cancer. She never had a chance, but she knew that from the start, and we gave her a good funeral, anyway, we gave her a steel coffin."

"Steel is better, I guess."

"Much better. You see, wood rots, and steel lasts. My sister never had a home of her own and she always wanted one, so we gave her the steel. I'm glad we did."

He might have made a good waiter but clearly he was cut out to have been an undertaker's assistant. Marjorie wondered again what made him become a brother. Probably some sermon on religious vocations when he was very young. Or maybe a priest who'd taken an interest in him at school, seen a good soul that might be made better. That was what religion did. It gave good men a quality that enhanced their goodness, gave them a kind of style. And it gave the mediocre man a choice—which was the real attraction of the Church, according to Harry. It offered a man the boldest possible choice, dared to suggest that you could give up everything for God, absolutely everything. And if you gave up that God of Catholicism it was really everything you gave up. Marjorie remembered how, at the beginning, she'd suspected that the Church was her big attraction for Harry; later on she was convinced of it. That elegant ideal of pure discipline there in the background was, as much as anything, what he'd married her for and it was, as much as anything, the reason he turned against her, the reason she gave him. She'd made the wrong choice, she was no longer what had attracted him, no longer, it sometimes seemed to her, anything specific, just a collection of habits, traits of mind, characteristics, all of it adding up to someone who was far more serious than anyone ever took her to be, really rather hopeless, but privately, and of necessity, pretty durable; intolerant, too, and yet insanely (Harry used to say) polite. She took a step back and said, "Well, I just wanted to thank you, Brother, for being so faithful."

"Tomorrow's the big day," he said. "Twenty-six priests will be on the altar concelebrating. They put an announcement on the bulletin board and twenty-six signed up; the most we ever had was thirty, and that was for the vice-provincial, Father McCabe. He died a year and a half ago. I had some job getting the chapel ready."

"You take care of that, too?"

He smiled proudly. "I'm sacristan. Would you like to see the way we set things up?"

"I wouldn't want to put you to that trouble," Marjorie said firmly.

"No trouble at all. Get your coat, we'll go on over."

She was certain someone would stop her and ask where she was off to and say she couldn't be spared, but the timing was against her. The evening was really getting started, and in the general coming and going Marjorie was able to cross the room, get her coat, and follow the brother into the corridor and out of the building without being noticed. It was snowing again. She kept slipping on the icy pavement and tasting snowflakes when she opened her mouth to speak —though there was hardly any need to say anything. Brother Desnoes was too excited and happy to listen or to care, and when they stepped into the basement of the chapel he was too busy. Wooden lockers lined the walls of the room, and the lockers were lined with chasubles—white, purple, green, gold; silk or fine wool with crosses or liturgical designs in gold thread or in velvet. "Lovely," Marjorie said as he dashed about, like a child showing off his playroom. "Lovely, Brother. Beautiful. Lovely."

"This is all new stuff, all modern. They don't wear the

old-type brocade anymore. Some of them don't use vestments at all when they say Mass." He shook his head angrily. "They come out on the altar in an old shirt or a sweater." He banged open another door and began pulling out drawer after tiny drawer. "Here's your amices," he said. "That's the little piece of linen they wear around the neck. Each one has his own set, and I make sure they're fresh. You have to change them, don't you know, every couple of days." He pushed on, calling her attention to chalices, cruets, ciboria —shelf upon shelf of them; a closetful of monstrances. "See this?" He picked up an elaborate gold chalice. "The Pope used it when he was here in '36—Pope Pius, only he was Cardinal then." Nothing the brother did was irreverent, but if his air of authority hadn't been so totally unconscious it would have seemed diabolically cool. Then he chose a key from among the others on his chain, and his manner became confidential. "How would you like to see the relic of the true Cross?"

Marjorie was horrified. "Brother, no!"

"It's right here." He unlocked a special little cupboard and took out the relic, seen on so many Good Fridays (lips touched to the figure that had just been wiped free of another kiss). "Take it, hold it."

She found herself grinning ridiculously, hefting the silver crucifix with the glass insert. How small it was, how light, how—yes—pretty. "Thank you, Brother," she said.

He took it and put it away. "Let's have a look up here." He opened a door on a narrow staircase that turned out to lead right up to the main altar—a huge altar, for the chapel was originally a parish church that the university had been built around. Brother Desnoes genuflected heavily, picked himself heavily up again, and made his way through a crisscross of wires that were attached to electric heaters there in the sanctuary and in all three aisles. "How's it going, Jack?" he called to one of the workmen in green overalls.

"O.K., Brother."

"Do we need any more heaters?"

"No, I think we're O.K."

Marjorie felt like someone who'd wandered onto a stage. Though it was an empty stage and she was only a sightseer, some exceptional response seemed to be required of her, but her only response was no response. She could only look around—at the huge marble altar, at the room-size Oriental carpet in front of it, at the stained-glass windows of the Jesuit martyrs, here in this Jesuit house given places of honor. She faced the body of the church, and something struck her then: the place where the rows of pews were and the sanctuary where she was standing seemed to be the same size, though when you were down in the pews the altar seemed so small and such a long way off. It was a perfectly pointless observation, and it depressed her to think that was all she could come up with, something trivial and irrelevant, something that wasn't even interesting.

Brother Desnoes picked his way back through the wires. "We have to start warming the place up tonight," he explained. "Otherwise you wouldn't be able to stand it in here tomorrow."

Marjorie nodded. There was an excuse to keep quiet— they were in church, after all—but she couldn't have said anything anyway. She felt too awful, too lonely for words, too lost and, above all, sorry. It was a while since she'd touched this particular base of feeling, but she knew perfectly well where she was and she was shocked to find herself there—at that point where the worst is over and you've discovered you're still on your feet, at the very beginning of the very end of love.

A low roar, like the sound of a cocktail party, was coming from the little room in the Administration Building and from the corridor outside, where some of the people were forced to congregate. The whole place seemed comfortable and cheerful, and Marjorie was almost glad to be back. She hung up her coat and turned to the crowd and saw the curly black back of her sister Caroline's head on the other side of the room. She'd started over in that direction when she picked up the sound of her mother's voice.

". . . and as soon as I stepped into that room I thanked God I'd come, because there was death in his face if ever I saw it. I went over to the bed, and his head moved, as if he were trying to tell me he knew me, so I began talking to him. 'You're the best brother in the world,' I said. 'I love you dearly, Jim, and I'm not going to let anything happen to you, but you've got to help. You've got to relax and forget about everything and everybody, though I know that's hard for you. You're always thinking of others,' I said, and that was the truth. All his life, he gave to others unstintingly and in the end he gave his very life for others."

The voice broke. The story had come to the right conclusion, and it was more than right, Marjorie thought. It was true. In acceptable ways and unacceptable ways Father Jim Murray had been always thinking of others. And one way or another he *had* given up his life for others—given it up as a young man to become a priest and then, possibly, realized what he'd given up and wondered why and tried to put up a fight against the life he'd chosen, or against himself, and eventually stopped wondering, stopped fighting, just went on with what he'd begun. And he had given up his last day to others, literally given his life to people who meant little or nothing to him, as though his life meant little or nothing, as though it were something he had no real use for. That was what had occurred to Marjorie when she walked into the hospital room. Eventually she'd been called; she got there just in time; and that was what struck her when she saw him lying in the hospital bed—what an ornamental thing his or anyone's life was, what a fanciful piece of workmanship compared to the pure and simple fact of dying.

The white hood that was part of the oxygen tent had fitted over the sick man's head like the hood certain monks wear when they come out to say Mass, and it had made him look very much a priest, an ascetic. Though he'd also looked very much a man—a man besieged, by the infection in his body and by the demands of his sister's talk. *You're the most generous, most loving fellow in the world, and I'm not going to let anything happen to you. What would we do without you? We can't do without you. We're not going to. . . .*

Most of the nurses at the hospital knew him, from all his visits to his men who'd been there. They kept looking in on him, and finally one capable, sensible little gray-haired woman came over to Marjorie and said, "Try and get your mother to stop talking for a while; it's bad for him." Marjorie did as she was told. Her mother did, too—she stopped talking, and it appeared then that she'd been holding on to him. When she let go, after a few minutes he let go, too, with a little sigh of relief.

Life After
Death

Yesterday evening I passed one of President Kennedy's sisters in the street again. They must live in New York—and in this neighborhood—the sister I saw and one of the others. They're good-looking women with a subdued, possibly unconscious air of importance that catches your attention. Then you recognize them. I react to them in the flesh the way I've reacted over the years to their pictures in the papers. I feel called on to account for what they do with their time, as if it were my business as well as theirs. I find myself captioning these moments when our paths cross. *Sister of the late President looks in shop window. Sister of slain leader buys magazine. Kennedy kin hails taxi on Madison Avenue.* And yesterday: *Kennedy sister and friend wait for light to change at Sixty-eighth and Lexington.* That was the new picture I added to the spread that opens out in my mind under the headline "LIFE AFTER DEATH."

It was beautifully cold and clear yesterday, and sunny and windless, so you could enjoy the cold without having to fight it, but I was dressed for the worst, thanks to my mother. At three o'clock she called to tell me it was bitter out, and though her idea of bitter and mine aren't the same, when I went outside I wore boots and put on a heavy sweater under my coat. I used to be overwhelmed by my mother's love; now it fills me with admiration. I've learned what it means to keep on loving in the face of resistance, though the resistance my two sisters and I offered wasn't to the love itself but to its superabundance, too much for our reasonable natures to cope with. My mother should have had simple, good-hearted daughters, girls who'd tell her everything, seated at the kitchen table, walking arm in arm with her in and out of department stores. But Grace and Rosemary and I aren't like that, not simple at all, and what goodness of heart we possess is qualified by the disposition we inherited from our father. We have a sense of irony that my mother with the purity of instinct and the passion of innocence sees as a threat to our happiness and thus to hers. Not one of us is someone she has complete confidence in.

Grace, the oldest of us, is married and has six children and lives in another city. Grace is a vivid person—vivid-looking with her black hair and high color, vivid in her strong opinions, her definite tastes. And Grace is a perfectionist who day after day must face the facts—that her son, Jimmy, never opens a book unless he has to and not always then; that her daughter Carolyn has plenty of boyfriends but no close girlfriends; that just when she gets a new refrigerator the washing machine will break down, then the dryer, then the house will need to be painted. My mother tells Grace that what can't be cured must be endured, but any such attitude would be a betrayal of Grace's ideals.

My middle sister, Rosemary, is about to marry a man of another religion. Rosemary is forty and has lived in Brussels and Stuttgart and Rome and had a wonderful time everywhere. No one thought she'd ever settle down, and my mother is torn between relief at the coming marriage and a new anxiety—just as she's torn, when Rosemary cooks

Christmas dinner, between pleasure and irritation. Rosemary rubs the turkey with butter, she whips the potatoes with heavy cream; before Rosemary is through, every pot in the kitchen will have been used. This is virtue carried to extremes and no virtue at all in the eyes of my mother, whose knowledge of life springs from the same homely frame of reference as my sister's but has led to a different sort of conclusion: Rubbed with margarine the turkey will brown perfectly well; to bring the unbeliever into the fold, you needn't go so far as to marry him.

Every so often I have a certain kind of dream about Mother—a dream that's like a work of art in the way it reveals character and throws light on situations. In one of these dreams she's just died—within minutes. We're in the house where I grew up, which was my grandmother's house. There are things to be done, and Grace and Rosemary and I are doing them, but the scene is one of lethargy, of a reluctance to get moving that belongs to adolescence, though in the dream, as in reality, my sisters and I are grown women. Suddenly I realize that Mother, though still dead, has got up and taken charge. There's immense weariness but no reproach in this act. It's simply that she's been through it all before, has helped bury her own mother and father and three of her brothers. She knows what has to be done but she's kept this grim knowledge from Grace and Rosemary and me. She's always tried to spare the three of us, with the result that we lack her sheer competence, her strength, her powers of endurance, her devotedness. In another dream Mother is being held captive in a house the rest of us have escaped from and can't get back into. We stand in the street, helpless, while inside she's being beaten for no reason. The anguish I feel, the tears that wake me are not so much for the pain she's suffering as for the fact that this should be happening to her of all people, someone so ill-equipped to make sense of it. Harshness of various kinds and degrees has been a continuing presence and yet a continuing mystery to her, the enemy she's fought blindly all her life. "I don't think that gray coat of yours is warm enough," she said to me yesterday.

"Sure it is," I said.

"It isn't roomy enough." As she spoke, she'd have been throwing her shoulders back in some great imaginary blanket of a coat she was picturing on me.

"It fits so close, the wind can't get in," I explained. "That's its great virtue."

"Let me give you a new coat," she said.

When I was four years old I had nephrosis, a kidney disease that was almost unheard of and nearly always fatal then. It singled me out. I became a drama, then a miracle, then my mother's special cause in life. From this it of course follows that I should be living the life she'd have liked for herself—a life of comfort—but desire has always struck me as closer to the truth of things than comfort could ever be. "I don't really want a new coat," I told her yesterday. "I like my gray one."

"Dress warmly when you go out," she said. "It's bitter cold."

As I was hanging up there was an explosion—down the street from me, half a block on either side of Lexington Avenue is being reconstructed. The School for the Deaf and the local Social Services Office were torn down, and now in place of those old, ugly buildings, battered into likenesses of the trouble they'd tried to mend, there are two huge pits where men drill and break rocks and drain water, yelling to each other like industrious children in some innovative playground. And all day long there are these explosions. There was another; then the phone rang again. It was Francis, for the second time that day. "Constance," he said. "What a halfwit I am."

I said, "You are?"

He gave the flat, quick, automatic laugh I hate, knowing it to be false. When Francis truly finds something funny, he silently shakes his head. "Yes, I am," he said. "I'm a halfwit. Here I made an appointment with you for tomorrow afternoon and I just turned the page of my calendar and found I've got some sort of affair to go to."

"What sort of affair?" I asked. It could have been anything from a school play to a war. Francis produces documentaries for television. He's also married and has four sons, two of them grown. He's a popular man, a man everyone loves, and when I think of why, I think of his face, his expression, which is of someone whose prevailing mood is both buoyant and sorrowful. He has bright brown eyes. His mouth is practically a straight line, bold and pessimistic. He has a long nose and a high forehead and these give his face severity, but his thick, curly, untidy gray-blond hair softens the effect.

"I'm down for some sort of cocktail party," he said. "This stupid, busy life of mine," he added.

This life of his, in which I figure only marginally, is an epic of obligation and entertainment. Work, eat, drink, and be merry is one way of putting it. It could also be put, as Francis might, this way: Talent, beauty, charm, taste, money, art, love—these are the real good in life, and each of these goods borrows from the others. Beauty is the talent of the body. Charm and taste must sooner or later come down to money. Art is an aspect of love, and love is a variable. And all this being, to Francis's way of thinking, so —our gifts being contingents—we can do nothing better than pool them. Use me, use each other, he all but demands. I say, no—we're none of us unique, but neither are we interchangeable. "Well, if you've got something else to do, Francis," I said to him yesterday, "I guess you'd better do it."

He said, "Why don't I come by the day after tomorrow instead?"

I said, "I'm not sure."

"Not sure you're free or not sure you want to?"

"Both." I wasn't exactly angry or hurt. I have no designs on Francis Hughes, no claim on him. It would be laughable if I thought I did.

"Ah," he said, "Inconstance."

I said, "No, indefinite."

He said, "Well, I'm going to put Thursday down on my calendar and I'll call you in the morning and see how you feel about it."

"All right," I said, but on Thursday morning I won't be here—if people aren't interchangeable, how much less so are people and events.

"Tell me you love me," said Francis.

I said, "I do."

He said, "I'll talk to you Thursday."

"Goodbye, Francis," I said, and I hung up and put on my boots and my heavy sweater and my gray coat and went out.

The college I went to is a few blocks from this brownstone where I have an apartment. It's a nice school, and I was happy there and I can feel that happiness still, as though these well-kept streets, these beautiful houses are an account that was held open for me here. But New York has closed out certain other accounts of mine, such as the one over in the West Fifties. Down one of those streets is the building where I used to work and where I first knew Francis. His office was across the hall from mine. His life was an open book, a big, busy novel in several different styles—part French romance, part character study, part stylish avant-garde, part nineteenth-century storytelling, all plot and manners, part Russian blockbuster, crammed with characters. His phone rang constantly. He had streams of visitors. People sent him presents—plants, books, cheeses, bottles of wine, boxes of English crackers. I was twenty-two or three at the time, but I saw quite clearly that the man didn't need more love, that he needed to spend some of what he'd accumulated, and being twenty-two or three I saw no reason why I shouldn't be the one to make that point. Or rather, what should have put me off struck me as reason for going ahead—for the truth is I'm not Francis's type. The girls who came to see him were more or less voluptuous, more or less blonde, girls who looked as if they were ready to run any risk, whereas I'm thin, and my hair is brown, and the risks I run with Francis are calculated, based on the fact that the love of someone like me can matter to someone like him only by virtue of its being in doubt. And having, as I say, no designs, I find myself able to be as hard on him as if he meant very little to me when, in fact, he means the world. I try now to avoid the West Fifties. Whenever I'm in that part of the city, the present seems lifeless, drained of all intensity in relation to that lost time when my days were full of Francis, when for hours on end he was close by.

I also try to avoid Thirty-fourth Street, where my father's brother-in-law used to own a restaurant, over toward Third Avenue. Flynn's was the name of it, and when I was twelve my father left the insurance business to become manager of Flynn's. He's an intelligent man, a man who again and again redeems himself with a word, the right word he's hit on effortlessly. His new raincoat, he told me the other day, "creaks." I asked if there was much snow left after a recent storm, and he said only a "batch" here and there. Sometimes he hits on the wrong word and only partly accidentally. "Pompadour," he was always calling French Premier Pompidou. He also has a perfect ear and a loathing for the current cliché. He likes to speak, with cheery sarcasm, of his "life-style." He also likes to throw out the vapid "Have a good day!" "No way" is an expression that simply drives him crazy.

The other night I dreamed a work of art about my father. He was in prison, about to be executed for some crime having to do with money. Rosemary and my mother and I had tried everything, but we failed to save him. At the end we were allowed—or obliged—to sit with him in his cell, sharing his terror and his misery and his amazing pluck. For it turned out that he'd arranged to have his last meal not at night but in the morning—so he'd have it to look forward to, he said. I woke up in despair. My father's spirit is something I love, as I love his sense of language, but common sense is more to the point in fathers, and mine has hardly any. As for business sense—after eight months at Flynn's, it was found that he'd been tampering with the books; six thousand dollars was unaccounted for. No charges were pressed, but my father went back to the insurance business, and from then on we didn't meet his family at Christmas and Easter, they didn't come to any more graduations or to Grace's wedding, Rosemary no longer got a birthday check from Aunt Kay Flynn, her godmother. You could say those people disappeared from our lives except that they didn't, at least not from mine. Once, when I was shopping with some friends in a department store, I spotted my Aunt Dorothy, another of my father's sisters. She was looking at skirts with my cousins Joan and Patricia, who are Grace's age —I must have been about sixteen at the time. A couple of summers later I had a job at an advertising agency where my cousin Bobby Norris turned out to be a copywriter. He was a tall, skinny, good-natured fellow, and he used to come and talk to me, and once or twice he took me out to lunch. He never showed any hard feelings toward our family, and neither did he seem to suspect how ashamed of us I was. Around this time I began running into my cousin Paul Halloran, who was my own age. At school dances and at the

Biltmore, where everybody used to meet, he'd turn up with his friends and I with mine. Then one Christmas I got a part-time job as a salesgirl at Altman's. A boy I knew worked in the stockroom, and sometimes we went for coffee after work, and once he asked me to have a drink. We were walking down Thirty-fourth Street when he told me where we were going—a bar that he passed every day and that he wanted me to inspect with him. Too late to back out, I realized he was taking me to Flynn's. As soon as I walked in, I saw my father's brother-in-law sitting at a table, talking to one of the waiters. He didn't recognize me, but I couldn't believe he wouldn't. I'm the image of my mother and I was convinced this would have to dawn on him, and that he'd come over and demand to know if I was who he thought I was, and so I drank my whiskey sour sitting sideways in the booth, one hand shielding my face, like a fugitive from justice. Or like the character in a movie who, when shot, will keep on going, finish the business at hand, and then keel over, dead.

It's three blocks north and three blocks east from the house where I live to the building where I went to college. Sometimes, of an afternoon, I work there now, in the Admissions Office, and yesterday I had to pick up a check that was due me. The Admissions Office is in a brownstone. The school has expanded. Times have changed. On the way in I met Sister Catherine, who once taught me a little biology. "Is it going to snow?" she asked.

I said, "It doesn't look like snow to me."

In the old days these nuns wore habits with diamond-shaped headpieces that made them resemble figures on playing cards, always looking askance. Yesterday Sister Catherine had on a pants suit and an imitation-fur jacket with a matching hat on her short, curly gray hair, and it was I who gave the sidelong glance, abashed in the face of this flowering of self where self had for so long been denied.

"It's cold enough for snow," Sister Catherine said.

I said, "It certainly is," and fled inside.

The house was adapted rather than converted into offices, which is to say the job was only half done. Outside Admissions there's a pullman kitchen—stove, sink, cabinets, refrigerator, dishes draining on a rack. Food plays an important part in the life of this office, probably because the clerical staff is made up of students who, at any given moment, may get the urge for a carton of yogurt, or a cup of soup, or an apple, or a can of diet soda. I went and stood in the doorway of the room where they sit: Delia, Yeshi, Eileen, Maggie. They knew someone was there, but no one looked up. They always wait to make a move until they must, and then they wait to see who'll take the initiative. One reason they like it when I'm in the office is that I can be counted on to reach for the phone on the first ring, to ask at once if I can help the visitor. But the routine of Admissions is complicated; every applicant seems to be a special case, and I work there on such an irregular basis that I can also be counted on not to be able to answer the simplest questions, and this makes the students laugh, which is another reason they like having me around. That someone like me, someone who's past their own inherently subordinate phase of life, should come in and stuff promotional material into envelopes, take down telephone requests for information, type up lists and labels —and do none of this particularly well—cheers them. I stepped into the office and said, "Hello, everybody." They stopped everything. I said, "Guess what I want."

"You want your check," said Yeshi, who comes from Ethiopia—the cradle of mankind. Lately I've been studying history. A friend of mine who's an Egyptologist lent me the text of a survey course, and now there are these facts lodged in my mind among the heaps of miscellaneous information accumulating there. "Where is Constance's check?" asked

Yeshi. She speaks with a quaver of a French accent. Her hands are tiny, her deft brown fingers as thin as pencils. She has enormous eyes. "Who made out Constance's time sheet?" she asked.

Maggie said, "I did." She wheeled her chair over to the file cabinet where the checks are kept. "It should be here. I'm sure I saw it this morning with the others." Maggie is Haitian. Her hair is cut close and to the shape of her head. She has a quick temper, a need to be listened to, and a need, every bit as great, to receive inspiration. "Uh-oh," she said.

"Not there?" I asked.

"It's got to be. I made out that time sheet myself," said Maggie. "I remember it was on Thursday—I'm not in on Wednesdays, and Friday would have been too late."

I said, "Well, I don't suppose anyone ran off with it. It was only for a few dollars."

"Money is money around here." This came from Delia, a pre-med student and the brightest of the girls. Her wavy light-brown hair hangs below her waist. She has prominent features—large hazel eyes, an almost exaggeratedly curved mouth, and a nose that manages to be both thin and full; but there's a black-haired, black-eyed sister, the beauty of the family, and so Delia must make fun of her own looks. She's Puerto Rican and must also make fun of that. She speaks in sagas of self-deprecation that now and again register, with perfect pitch, some truth of her existence. "There's no poor like the student poor," she said yesterday.

"That's a fact, Delia," I said. "But I don't plan on contributing my wages to the relief of the Student Poor."

Maggie began pounding the file cabinet. "I made out that time sheet *myself*. I brought it in *myself* and had Mrs. Keene sign it; then I took it right over to the business office and handed it to feebleminded Freddy. He gave me a hard time because it wasn't with the others. I hate that guy." She pounded the cabinet again.

Yeshi said, "Maybe Mrs. Keene has it."

"Is she in her office?" I could see for myself by stepping back; Olivia was at her desk.

"Come on in," she called.

I said to the students, "I'll be back," and I went to talk to my friend.

"You're just in time for tea and strumpets," she said.

Olivia was in school with me here, but her name then was McGrath. She's been married and divorced and has two sons, and I say to myself, almost seriously, that the troubled course of her life must be the right course since it's given her the name Keene, which describes her perfectly. She's clever, capable, resilient, dresses well, wears good jewelry, leads a busy life. Except for the divorce, Olivia is an example of what my mother would like me to be, though her own mother continually finds fault. "I wonder what it's like to be proud of your children," Mrs. McGrath will say.

Olivia reached for the teapot on her desk and said, "Have a cup."

"No thanks," I said. "I only came by to pick up my check, but it doesn't seem to be outside."

She opened her desk drawer, fished around, and came up with a brown envelope. "Someone must have put it here for safest keeping." She handed me the envelope and said, "Come on, sit down for a minute. Hear the latest outrage."

I sat down in the blue canvas chair beside the desk. I love offices and in particular that office, where the person I am has very little fault to find with the person I was. I begin to wonder, when I'm there, whether the movement of all things isn't toward reconciliation, not division. I'm half convinced that time is on our side, that nothing is ever lost, that we need only have a little more faith, we need only believe a little more and the endings will be happy. Grace's children will be a credit to her. Rosemary will find herself living in a style in keeping with her generous nature. My mother will come to trust the three of us. Olivia's mother will learn to appreciate Olivia. Francis will see how truly I love him. I'll be able to walk down Thirty-fourth Street and not give it a thought. "All right," I said to Olivia, "let's hear the latest outrage."

"Yesterday was High School Day."

"How many came?" I asked.

"A record hundred and seventy, of whom one had her gloves stolen, five got stuck in the elevator, and twelve sat in on a psychology class where the visiting lecturer was a transsexual."

"Oh God," I said.

"Tomorrow I get twelve letters from twelve mothers and dads."

"Maybe they won't tell their parents." I never told mine about seeing Aunt Dorothy shopping for skirts, or about the time I went to Flynn's for a drink, or how my first boyfriend, Gene Kirk, tried to get me to go to bed with him. To this day, I tell people nothing. No one knows about Francis.

Olivia said, "Nowadays kids tell all. Last week Barney came home and announced that his teacher doesn't wear a bra."

I looked at the two little boys in the picture on Olivia's desk. "How old is Barney?" I asked.

"Ten."

He has blond hair that covers his ears, and light-brown eyes with a faraway look. He calls the office and says, "Can I speak to Mrs. Keene? It's me." His brother, Bartholomew, is a couple of years older. Like Olivia, Bart has small, neat features and an astute expression. He sometimes does the grocery shopping after school. He'll call the office and discuss steaks and lamb chops with his mother, and I remember how when I was a little older than he I used to have to cook supper most evenings. The job fell to me because Grace wasn't at home—she'd won a board-and-tuition scholarship

to college—and Rosemary was studying piano, which kept
her late most evenings, practicing or at her lessons. And
after my father's trouble at Flynn's my mother had to go
back to teaching music herself. She's a good—a born—
musician, but the circumstances that made her take it up
again also made her resent it. I resented it, too, because of
what it did to my life. After school, I'd hang around till the
last minute at the coffee shop where everyone went; then I'd
rush home and peel the potatoes, shove the leftover roast in
the oven or make the ground beef into hamburgers, heat the
gravy, set the table—all grudgingly. But Bartholomew
Keene takes pride in his shopping and so does Olivia. In our
time, people have made trouble manageable. I sat forward
and said, "I'd better get going."

"Think of it," said Olivia. "A transsexual."

I said, "Put it out of your mind."

In the main office, the students were in a semi-demoral-
ized state. Their feelings are in constant flux; anything can
set them up or down, and though they work hard, they work
in spurts. My turning up was an excuse to come to a halt.
I showed them my pay envelope. Maggie pounded the desk
and said, "I *knew* it had to be around here somewhere."

"And I believed in you, Maggie," I said.

" 'I be-lieve for ev-ry drop of rain that falls,' " sang Delia,
" 'a flow-er grows.' " They love to sing—when they're tired,
when they're fresh, when they're bored or happy or upset.

" 'I be-lieve in mu-sic!' " Maggie snapped her fingers,
switching to the rock beat that comes naturally to them.
Eileen got up and went into her dance—she's a thin, pretty
blonde with a sweet disposition and the soul of a stripper.

" 'I be-lieve in mu-sic!' " they all yelled—all except Yeshi,
who only smiled. Yeshi is as quiet as the others are noisy but
she loves their noise. Noise gives me eyestrain. I began
backing off.

"When are you coming in again?" asked Delia.

I said, "Next week, I think."

Yeshi laughed. Her full name is Yeshimebet. Her sisters are named Astair, Neghist, Azeb, Selamawit, and Etsegenet. Ethiopia lies between Somalia and the Sudan on the Red Sea, whose parting for Moses may have been the effect of winds on its shallow waters.

After I left the office yesterday, I went to evening Mass. I often do. I love that calm at the end of the day. I love the routine, the prayers, the ranks of monks in their white habits, who sit in choir stalls on the altar—I go to a Dominican church, all gray stone and vaulting and blue stained glass. Since it's a city parish, my companions at Mass are diverse —businessmen and students and women in beautiful fur coats side by side with nuns and pious old people, the backbone of congregations. I identify myself among them as someone who must be hard to place—sometimes properly dressed, sometimes in jeans, not so much devout as serious, good-looking but in some undefined way. It's a true picture of me but not, of course, the whole truth. There's no such thing as the whole truth with respect to the living, which is why history appeals to me. I like the finality. Whatever new finds the archeologists may make for scholars to dispute, the facts stand. Battles have been won or lost, civilizations born or laid waste, and the labor and sacrifice entailed are over, can perhaps even be viewed as necessary or at least inevitable. The reasons I love the Mass are somewhat the same. During those twenty or so minutes, I feel my own past to be not quite coherent but capable of eventually proving to be that. And if my life, like every other, contains elements of the outrageous, that ceremony of death and transfiguration is a means of reckoning with the outrageousness, as work and study are means of reckoning with time.

Yesterday Father Henshaw said the five-o'clock Mass. He doesn't linger over the prayers—out of consideration, you can tell, for these people who've come to church at the end of a day's work—but he's a conscientious priest and he places his voice firmly on each syllable of each word as he addresses God on behalf of us all, begging for pardon, mercy, pity, understanding, protection, love. By the time Mass was over yesterday, the sun had set, and as I stepped onto the sidewalk I had the feeling I was leaving one of the side chapels for the body of the church. The buildings were like huge, lighted altars. The sky was streaked with color—a magnificent fresco, too distant for the figures to be identified. The rush hour had started. The street was crowded with people—flesh-and-blood images, living tableaux representing virtue and temptation: greed on one face, faith on another, on another charity, or sloth, fortitude, or purity. And there, straight out of Ecclesiastes, I thought—vanity of vanities, all is vanity. Then I realized I was looking at President Kennedy's sister. She was with a dark-haired man in a navy-blue overcoat. I had the impression at first that he was one of the Irish cousins, but I changed my mind as she smiled at him. It was a full and formal smile, too full and formal for a cousin and for that drab stretch of Lexington Avenue. It was a smile better given at official receptions to heads of state, and I got a sense, as I walked behind the couple, of how events leave people stranded, how from a certain point in our lives on—a different point for each life —we seem only to be passing time. I thought of the Kennedys in Washington, the Kennedys in London, the Kennedys in Boston and Hyannis Port. Which were the important days? The days in the White House? The days at the Court of St. James's? Or had everything that mattered taken place long before, on the beaches of Cape Cod where we saw them sailing and swimming and playing games with one another?

We reached the corner of Sixty-eighth and had to wait for the light to change. It's a busy corner, with a subway station, a newsstand, a hot-dog stand, and a flower stand operated by a man and his wife. The flower sellers are relative newcomers to the corner. I began noticing them last summer, when they were there all day, but when winter came they took to setting up shop in late afternoon. For the cold they dress alike in parkas, and boots, and trousers, and gloves with the fingers cut out. They have the dark features of the Mediterranean countries and they speak to each other in a foreign language. They have a little boy who's almost always with them. I'd guess he's about five, though he's big for five, but at the same time he also seems young for whatever age he may be, possibly because he appears to be so contented on that street corner. A more sophisticated child might sulk or whine or get into trouble, but not that little boy. Sometimes he has a toy with him—a truck or an airplane or a jump rope. He also has a tricycle that he rides when the weather is good. If it's very cold he may shelter in the warmth of the garage a few doors down from the corner, or he'll sit in his parents' old car, surrounded by flowers that will replenish the stock as it runs out. In hot weather, he sometimes stretches out on the sidewalk, but that's the closest I've ever seen him come to being at loose ends. He's a resourceful little boy, and he's independent like his parents, who work hard and for the most part silently. I've never seen them talking with the owner of the hot-dog stand or the newsdealer. Business is business on that corner, and not much of it comes from me. I never buy hot dogs, flowers only once in a blue moon, and newspapers not as a rule but on impulse. Yesterday, I put my hand in my pocket and found a dollar bill there and I decided to get a paper. I picked up a *Post* and put my money in the dealer's hand. As he felt through his pockets full of coins, the flower sellers' little boy suddenly appeared, dashed over to his parents' cart, seized a daisy, and put his nose to the yellow center. The newsdealer gave me three quarters back. The traffic lights changed. President Kennedy's sister started across the street. The flower seller's wife grabbed the daisy from her son, and he ran off. I put the quarters in my pocket and moved on.

Yesterday's headlines told of trouble in the Middle East —Israel of the two kingdoms, Israel and Judah; Iran that was Alexander's Persia; Egypt of the Pharaohs and the Ptolemies. I love those ancient peoples. I know them. They form a frieze, a band of images carved in thought across my mind —emperors, princesses, slaves, scribes, farmers, soldiers, musicians, priests. I see them hunting, harvesting, dancing, embracing, fighting, eating, praying. The attitudes are all familiar. The figures are noble and beautiful and still.

A Story in
the Key of C

"You make these pronouncements about me, and the truth is you don't know me at all," Joe Fletcher said to me last week, after three years of whatever this is—I'd have called it knowing each other.

"There isn't such a lot to know about anyone," I answered, meaning that the passions that drive us through life are the same in each of us, but Joe took my remark at face value.

"What shallow kind of talk is that?" he said angrily, and he got up and began walking around. We were in the living room of his house on Long Island. "This marvellous house," he'd called it a few minutes earlier. In my opinion that house leaves a lot to be desired, but houses often strike me that way. I'm a decorator. Joe and I met when I was working for some people named Morrison who live near him, though the Morrisons didn't introduce us—Joe doesn't know them. He came up to me himself one evening when I was alone on the beach. I thought he was the most agreeable man I'd ever met and I still think that, though I've learned that he's also inclined to be argumentative.

"Of course there's a lot to know about anyone," he said.

"But it all comes down to the same things—love, hate, hunger, fear, sickness, sorrow. Circumstances only ring the changes."

"Only!" he said.

"Would you say you know me?" I asked.

He hesitated and then conceded, "I have certain strong impressions."

I let it go at that, though I wondered why, of the two propositions—equally true, equally false, and equally obvious: that people are different, that people are the same— he'd defended the first, when on the evidence he himself has written off human nature in all its variety or predictability. He lives alone on the tip of the Island, loves his daughter but probably no one else, teaches at a small local college to avoid the encroachments on him that there'd be at a school with more of a name; he rolls his own cigarettes, grows his own vegetables in his own greenhouse, bakes his own bread, repairs his own car and anything else of his that breaks down —he's a scientist, a mathematician. Twenty years ago, when he was thirty-five, he made what was an important contribution to this dry discipline; he simplified some theorem, eliminated a step in some equation. This is a crowning achievement in the eyes of his colleagues, but Joe works ferociously on, indifferent to the question of success or failure. I love his integrity, his industry, but I love best of all his ordinariness. The sight of him in a navy-blue nylon turtleneck pullover thrills me. The sound of his long, deliberate, confidential (misleadingly so) "Yeah" takes my breath away. He is so on key—the key of C major. Intellectually Joe is in a class by himself, but in his speech, his dress, his mannerisms he's the common man, which is what I was getting at in my "pronouncement." "You're really so average," I'd said. "You could easily be living the most average life."

I meant it as a compliment, a high compliment at that.

I was brought up to be different, to be better, with the result that nothing appeals to me more than the common touch. But Joe's upbringing was an ambiguous affair. His mother was Italian, his father English. There was money in the family, but not the background that gives money its charm. There was love, too, but love that ran hot and cold and did more harm than good. Joe is sensitive about this whole picture—sensitive also about himself physically, being neither young nor handsome. Nor particularly well put together. He's too tall, which has given him a stoop. His bottom is thin, his back thick, his legs heavy. His features are well-proportioned, but his face has a haggard look. He once mentioned that he resembles his mother, but I think his expression must come from his English father, along with a certain stiffness, a refinement that he sometimes repudiates and sometimes indulges in himself. Most of the time, though, he favors the Italian side of his nature, the side that's given to angry outbursts but also to gestures of the purest sympathy.

He came over and sat down beside me on the sofa. "Are you blue?" he asked.

"No, I'm not blue," I said.

"Are you sure?"

"What would I have to be blue about?" I smiled as I said it, knowing the question wouldn't be answered, for we don't elaborate on our feelings—my feelings, that is; with respect to me, Joe is on the verge of feeling. I wait for him to falter in his self-sufficiency, to stumble into frailty, intimacy, love.

He said, "I'm hungry. What about you?"

It was a little after seven. I'd come out on the two o'clock train, skipping lunch, but I never feel like eating when I'm with Joe. He absorbs my appetites, leaving me indifferent to food or sleep or exercise. I said, "I'm not particularly hungry."

He was downcast. "Not particularly hungry?" My lack of

appetite seemed to take away his. He has an ideal of closeness that real men and women forever fall short of, and the
gradual realization of this over the years has driven him into
himself and made him uncommunicative. He loves to talk
on the phone, though. Distance brings down some barrier,
freeing the man I originally found so appealing. "Come back
to the house and let me make you some fried clams," he said
that first evening, as if we'd been running into each other
on the beach for years. The clams were delicious; Joe is a
good cook.

"I'm going to eat something, but what?" he asked himself
now, and went over to the kitchen. I could hear him keeping
up the half-conversation that he often lapses into—unfinished comments, unanswered questions, sometimes just
sounds. Solitude is his natural element, and I began to feel
extraneous, so I went out onto the deck. From Joe's house
you can see the ocean. It was perfectly calm that night, but
the sky was full of a raging sunset. The air was cold for the
middle of June. In a little while the door opened and he
handed me a sweater. Joe is sensible in the way another man
might be romantic. Where someone else will bring flowers
and pay compliments, he bestows sweaters and advice. He
looked out over the sea and up at the sky and then said, "It's
damp out here. You'll catch cold." It was no idle comment.
Accuracy is a passion with him, and he always means what
he says.

I went inside, thinking of the person I was before I knew
Joe, hardly recognizing myself. I used to live cautiously, love
carefully, measuring every move against a standard of emotional profit and loss, but Joe is beyond my powers of calcula-
tion. I love him and live dangerously, catching a train to be
with him at a moment's notice, arranging to be home when
I think he might call, bending over backwards not to make
him jealous, not to be the one to let the distance open up
between us. It's a daring course to pursue with someone as

mercurial as he is, and yet, if I were to describe the state of my heart that evening, I'd compare it to the calm sea rather than the turbulent sky. He's woken something new in me, a devotion I wouldn't have thought I was capable of—that I would, in fact, had I suspected myself of it three years ago, have wanted to disavow. Like most women I'd rather play the heroine than the supporting part, but even the mildest heroines must assert themselves, and difficult though Joe is he inspires me with the opposite of assertiveness—he is difficult out of need, difficult rather than be disappointed, rather than despair; he makes me forget myself.

I followed him to the kitchen and found that he'd fixed two sandwiches of homemade bread, homegrown lettuce and tomatoes. "They look delicious," I said. He sliced the sandwiches, put them on plates, and gave me one. "Don't you want it?" I asked.

He said, "No, it's for you. I made it for you." He poured two glasses of beer and shook some potato chips into a bowl, which he offered me, saying "Don't be shy" in an accent that was pure County Galway—Joe is, of all things, a mimic. I went laughing into the living room, back to the sofa. When he came in he settled himself in his dilapidated easy chair, halfway across the room. He's a bit nearsighted, which he ignores, being also a little vain. "What's the world been up to?" he said, and got up and turned the television on to the news.

"Up to no good," I said as the picture came into focus. A presidential candidate was being endorsed by a labor leader. Then a holdup victim came on and described his ordeal. Daniel Patrick Moynihan had given a commencement address that day, and afterwards he was interviewed by reporters. "Do you know who he reminds me of?" I called across to Joe.

"Who?"

"Barbara's boyfriend." Barbara is my sister.

Joe said, "What about him?"

I pointed to the screen. "Daniel Patrick Moynihan reminds me of Barbara's boyfriend." Family lore interests him, possibly because in his own family the past seems to wither away—for lack of cultivation, I'd say. When his parents died they were buried unceremoniously. One of his brothers lives in California, the other in London; both are childless, both divorced. Phone calls are rare among them, letters unheard of. That the Fletchers weren't happy could explain their disregard for family ties, but that explanation doesn't satisfy me. My own upbringing was a sorry mess— a broken home melodramatically patched and repatched, over and over—yet my parents and my sisters and I stick together, observing the festivals of our common life as faithfully as if nothing but good times bound us to one another. The truth is, love in families is more or less an effort that Joe, for whatever reasons, can't bring himself to make, though he's curious about our birthdays, wedding anniversaries, graduations, Christmases.

"When's your sister getting married?" he asked.

I said, for the hundredth time (he harps on this), "I don't know."

He shook his head. His own marriage must have been strained to the breaking point by this skepticism, for doesn't habitual expectation of the worst leave the door open to trouble? And on the other hand, isn't hope a prerequisite for happiness? I believe that's so, and it irritates me to have Joe voice his suspicions about my sister's admittedly long, drawn-out romance. "Barbara'd better watch her step," he said.

I said, "Don't worry about Barbara. Harry loves her."

"How do you know?" he asked, not so much doubting as requiring proof, but I had no equation to offer, no mathematical certitude—just human word, as unassailable or as full of holes as you'll let it be.

"He says so."

Joe shook his head again but this time with less conviction. Belief affects him. It disturbs him, rousing secret misgivings as to the hard stand he's taken on life. He wouldn't mind discovering he's wrong, but it isn't that easy. Belief is long, and Joe is impatient. He got up and brought his dishes out to the kitchen. I heard him tidying up—he's a meticulous man. His kitchen is spotless, his house immaculate. I took the last bite of my sandwich, drank the last of my beer, and brought him my plate and my glass. "Do you feel like going to a movie?" he asked. If he'd been in good spirits, he'd have suggested a walk along the beach.

I said, "What's playing?"

"I don't know." He shrugged and hooked his thumbs in his belt. He looked tired and forlorn, a man in sudden need of what he so systematically resists—a helping hand.

I went and got the newspaper and looked up the movie listings. "Some Robert Redford thing is at the R.K.O.," I called.

"Still? I saw that two weeks ago with Mary."

Mary is his daughter, a good-looking girl with features like Joe's but dark where he's fair. There are pictures of her all around the house: Mary at her high-school graduation holding a bouquet of roses, Mary as a very young child dressed in a rabbit costume, Mary bundled up in sweaters down on the beach by the water's edges, Mary in a long dress. He loves her without reserve, showering on her the affection and attention that he withholds from others, but Mary will soon be eighteen, and though she loves the beach she spends less and less time there.

I said, "Can you stand Robert Redford again? Not that I'm dying to see him."

"Then we'll stay put."

He turned off the kitchen light and came into the living room and began straightening things up. I amused myself,

as I often do, by refurnishing that room in my mind, clearing
out the assorted castoffs that Joe has assembled there and
replacing them with wicker chairs, tables made of unfinished
wood, striped canvas and flowered cotton slipcovers, grass
carpeting, straw blinds. But I wouldn't touch the battered
grand piano that stands against one wall, like an enormous
and beloved family pet. Joe had left some change on the
piano cover. He put the coins in his pocket and went around
to the keyboard and struck a couple of chords. When he was
twenty or so, he wanted to be a night-club piano player, and
he'd have been good at it. He has a straightforward style at
the piano and he has the manner—ruefully personable,
world-weary—of the best barroom musicians. He pulled out
the bench and sat down and began playing songs from the
nineteen forties. In those years he was a young man, a soldier
in the Second World War, and though his hair is completely
gray now, his face deeply lined, youth is what he still sug-
gests. Age has made him pessimistic but no less susceptible,
and this comes overwhelmingly across when he's at the
piano. "Easy Come, Easy Go," "Everything Happens to
Me," "I'll Never Smile Again," "Imagination," "Skylark"—
I was a child when those songs were popular, when the
young soldier was fighting in North Africa. Listening to him
play, I felt our lives touch in a way that was remote but
conclusive—we'd shared the fear and the danger of war-torn
times, when everything was threatened and everyone
seemed close. And we'd come through. I'd have liked to go
and sit beside him on the piano bench, marvelling with him
at our survival and at the happy chance of our paths having
crossed, but I knew he wouldn't appreciate it. So I stayed
where I was, thinking about him—about how exacting he is,
how ambivalent, how intense, how impulsive, how funny in
a serious sort of way, how realistic, how direct, how utterly
without affectation. I thought of his flat toes, his beautiful
teeth, his loud laugh, of the way he swings his arms when

he walks, closing his hands into fists. I know a lot about him, really. When he said I didn't, what he may have had in mind was the fact that he himself tells me very little. My knowledge is contraband, acquired by stealth when I'm with him, smuggled away on my person. I looked over at him. He was slouched at the keyboard, as if it were a desk full of papers. His eyes were half closed. He was in another world. He loves to play.

Dreaming

"**M**usic is something you'll always have," Mrs. Lynch told the children, Eileen and Kathleen. When Mr. Lynch questioned the cost of lessons, she said, "It's an investment." He looked away from her, remembering how the first time he laid eyes on her, she'd been sitting at the piano in a white dress with a red sash, her black hair tied back with a red ribbon. Loyal to that vision, though it had been misleading, he set aside his objections.

Thursdays at three-thirty, Mrs. Eberhardt rode up to the Lynches' in a taxicab, eased herself out, opened her expensive handbag and produced, almost invariably, a large bill for the cabdriver to change. Mrs. Eberhardt and her husband, who was a lawyer, lived on Central Park West and had a maid. Where another woman might have joined a club or taken up a cause, she gave piano lessons, her reasons having to do with spare time, some idea of being useful, and the sheer sociability that showed in her lively manner and in her clothes. She wore silk dresses, jewelry, pretty shoes, and always a hat with a veil which she left on during the lessons, drawing the veil up off her face, fixing it against the sparse

191

bush of her faded blonde hair. A dusting of face powder formed another fine veil over her lightly freckled skin. She had pale, clear eyes and a wide mouth with narrow lips. She counted out loud.

The winter Eileen Lynch was nine, she was playing minor scales, octaves and arpeggios, and "Skating on the Ice of Sweet Briar," a glittering showpiece with a glissando at the end. Mrs. Eberhardt had given Eileen a pin, enamel on sterling silver in the shape of a piano, black with red keys, which Eileen wore on weekends and in the afternoon when she came home from Holy Family School, jewelry being forbidden during school hours. "Beauty needs no adorning," the nuns said.

Kathleen, who was seven, coveted the piano pin and secretly tried it on, longing for one of her own. In her first winter of music, she played the C major, the G major and the D major scales. "Thumb under," Mrs. Eberhardt would call out in advance, throwing Kathleen off so that she missed the fourth beat altogether. If you struck a wrong note, Mrs. Eberhardt would find the guilty finger and set it on the right key. Kathleen's hand stiffened. "Loosen up!" Mrs. Eberhardt cried, holding out her own hands, shaking them from the wrist until the fingers flew. Kathleen was given pieces of three or four lines which the left hand and the right played alternately.

After the lessons, over a cup of tea, Mrs. Eberhardt spoke of her son, Helmut, who was an engineer. He had no interest in music—and neither did Sally, his wife, or Tom, Jane and Steven, their children. To Mrs. Lynch this was an unnatural and rather shocking state of affairs, in a class with abdication or apostasy, not to be taken as lightly as Mrs. Eberhardt seemed to. Looking for reassurance, she'd work the conversation around to her own girls. In Mrs. Eberhardt's opinion, Eileen had ability, and Kathleen showed promise.

Eileen learned "In an Eighteenth Century Drawing

Room," which was taken from Mozart's Sonata in C. Kathleen was given "Sunny Jim," which the two hands played simultaneously and which won her a piano pin, green with orange keys. She didn't care for the colors.

Mrs. Lynch, who'd been accumulating grounds for disappointment of her own, finally came to some conclusions. Mrs. Eberhardt was a lovely person, but Kathleen was making no progress, and Eileen had no repertoire. Furthermore, "In an Eighteenth Century Drawing Room" was not the real thing. She began to make inquiries, with the idea of changing teachers, and then happened to see a newspaper article about a settlement house with a marvellous music school. Theory and composition were taught, she told Mr. Lynch. Teachers from the Juilliard School gave their time for next to nothing. Mr. Lynch, who only liked music you could sing to or dance to or at least listen to, had come to a conclusion of his own—it would be some time before his investment realized any dividends he could appreciate. "Do what you think best," he said.

There were auditions at the settlement house in a narrow room with a piano against one wall and, on the opposite wall, a blackboard with painted staves. On heavy, straight-backed chairs sat Mr. Field, director of the music school, Miss Hoffman, one of the teachers, and Vicki Hana, Mr. Field's Japanese protégée from Juilliard. Eileen played "In an Eighteenth Century Drawing Room," and Kathleen did "Sunny Jim." They recognized, both of them, that they were in the presence of the real thing, and that it posed a threat. What was familiar, domestic, almost frivolous was turning into a discipline whose demands the children could scarcely imagine much less hope to meet. Mr. Field had cold blue eyes and curly hair that fell onto his forehead. He wasted no words. Miss Hoffman was plain-looking and had a supercilious air. Viki Hana—tiny, dignified, graceful, exotic— seemed to be there simply to confirm the impression that it was all very strange, possibly fantastic.

"We'll be in touch with you," Mr. Field said to Mrs. Lynch. Three weeks later, he wrote:

We are very pleased to place Eileen Lynch on our enrollment and are assigning her to Miss Chernoff, who is generally considered the finest teacher on the staff. Eileen will start in on Theory I. If the work is insufficiently stimulating, we propose to advance her.

We are also accepting your younger daughter. She will study with Miss Rosen who does especially well with beginners. We will try Kathleen in Theory I and see how she makes out.

Somewhere in the settlement house, there was always shouting going on. Doors were always being slammed. On the main floor, in the lobby, there were art exhibits, pictures done not with crayon but with paints, the colors slapped on, you could tell, with inspiration and fervor—maybe even genius. Behind the lobby, in the auditorium, classes were held in modern dance. Girls in tights flung themselves around or held some uncomfortable-looking pose they happened to fall into. It was all very different from Holy Family where silence and restraint were drummed in so constantly as to seem to prevail. In the opinion of the nuns, self-expression needed no encouragement. Noises heard in the corridor of Holy Family were faint, like the step of a solitary child on the stone stairs or on the wooden floor, going with a message from one classroom to another. Or there were solid, heavy sounds—a whole class tramping up or down stairs, or reciting the times table or a spelling lesson, or learning a hymn; bodies moving and voices being raised in unison—another kind of silence.

As for Art, the nuns met that obligation. Once a week, each class had a drawing lesson from Miss O'Shea. Guide lines were laid down, then the guide lines were darkened, then the colors put on, in crayon. Miss Fazio, the church organist, taught choral singing. (Monsignor Hayes, pastor of Holy Family, liked the children to be able to sing the Mass.) Miss Hanlon, who got up the school performance each year, taught tap and ballet on the side. Monsignor's secretary, Miss Leahy, was soloist with the adult choir and also took a few private voice pupils. Anything beyond those provisions the nuns might be willing to indulge, but when Eileen and Kathleen Lynch, in their separate classrooms, collected their books on Friday at half past two instead of three, slid out of their seats, went quietly to the cloakroom, put on their hats and coats and left, the nuns took no notice. And if any of the other children in the two classes watched, they were told, "Eyes front, please." Or, "Who gave anyone permission to look up from her work?"

The nuns and the music school were of different covenants, but in a certain sense they were related—linked, though opposed, in the manner of the two great traditions from which the settlement house and Holy Family each received its character, the Old Testament and the New. Speaking of this to Mr. Lynch, Mrs. Lynch said with humility, gratitude and wonder, "Out of a hundred and fifty students, our two are the only Christians."

If they'd made good time and got to the settlement house early, Mrs. Lynch always had errands that could be taken care of there in the Jewish neighborhood, where the shopwindows bore a mysterious legend, the word that looked to the little Lynches something like TWO. By the time they reached the settlement house, there was usually only a minute left for Eileen and Kathleen to get a look, as they went by the auditorium, at the modern dancing. "We're going to be late," Mrs. Lynch would say, opening a door onto the staircase that led to the upper floors.

The stairs were bright green and the bannisters royal blue. The walls of the stairwell were yellow. The door to the second floor was black and said "Music" in red letters. After the violence of those colors, the wide, dim music corridor was as dull as any classroom, as businesslike as any office. Just inside the door, in a little cubbyhole, sat Miss Ellenbogen, the registrar and bookkeeper, receiving payment and recording it in her ledger. Her hair, a soft shade of red, fascinated and puzzled Kathleen. How could someone have red hair and not be Irish?

Miss Rosen had pitch black hair, prominent eyes, and a full mouth. She was very tall and wore dark, tailored suits that had no style. She was enthusiastic and patient. *Keep wrists high,* she wrote in the notebook each pupil was required to buy. *Raise fingers. Attack!* Miss Rosen relied on the Diller-Quayle books where good taste could be counted on, even in Volume I which was given over to folk songs. "Make the melody sing!" Miss Rosen, urging Kathleen on, would sing out herself, with obvious enjoyment.

Miss Chernoff believed in the curved-hand position, fingers cupped low on the keys, wrists level with the fingers. She was in great demand at Juilliard and came to the settlement house late in the afternoon with an air of knowing, in all honesty, her own worth. Her hair, which she wore up, was always dropping from the pins. She dressed in bright colors —fuschia, gold, turquoise—but she was a stern disciplinarian. Once, during Eileen's lesson, she whirled around on her piano stool and demanded, "Who is drumming?" and Kathleen discovered that she'd been tapping her foot on the linoleum floor. After that, Kathleen brought a book to the music school and waited in the corridor during Eileen's lesson. Miss Chernoff thought highly of the Diller-Quayle books but she used them only as a point of departure. Eileen began on Volume III and was soon into Bach Two-Part Inventions.

Miss Kahn, who taught theory, was a graduate of Columbia. She was lovely—pretty, soft-spoken, gentle, quite shy, and anxious not to appear cold, which gave her perfect

manners a purity and intensity that was echoed in the shades
of the wool dresses she wore: dark green, light blue, heather,
or navy with white collar and cuffs. The theory book,
"Learning to Listen," looked like a coloring book with its
soft covers and the picture on the front of three children
sitting on a settee, singing. Inside the book, pages of empty
staves waited to become music, with directions that were
explicit enough but proved difficult to grasp. *Draw picture
of up and down. Draw picture of long and short. Play by ear;
begin on C, then on G.* There were verses whose rhythmic
pattern was to be marked off, single lines of an incomplete-
ness Kathleen found irritating. Their content was an insult:

> I had a lit–tle nut tree, noth–ing would it bear.
> Pret–ty Phyl–lis, will you dance with me the light ga–votte?
> Nee–dles and pins! nee–dles and pins!

Eileen was taken from Theory I and put into Theory II.

Out in the wide corridor, parents and children came and
went and waited. Doors opened and closed. Chords escaped,
cries for help which Kathleen ignored as she read in "Old
French Fairy Tales" of Princess Blondine, left in the forest
by her wicked stepmother and befriended there by a superb
cat, Beau Minon, and a pretty white hind, Bonne Biche. Of
Princess Rosette whose only clothes—a percale robe, cotton
stockings, black shoes and a barette—become, when she
dresses to go to the ball, a gown of gold brocade, white satin
shoes with buckles of one single ruby of wonderful splendor,
stockings as fine as a spider's web, and a headdress of dia-
monds, each the size of a walnut. And of Prince Ourson,
born through a fairy's curse with skin as hairy as a bear's.
Through the love of his sweet cousin, Violette, the spell is
broken. By her tears, Ourson's fur is washed away. They
marry and have eight sons and four daughters, all of them
charming.

To tide Eileen and Kathleen over the long afternoons, Mrs. Lynch brought a thermos bottle of milk and soda cracker sandwiches of peanut butter and jelly or cream cheese and jelly. She herself loved those hours at the music school. She loved the spirit of dedication in the air, the spirit of study, of sacrifice, of hard-won satisfactions. The Jewish parents noticed her. When she brought out the thermos bottle and the soda cracker sandwiches they spoke of what a wonderful mother she was, which Mrs. Lynch took as a tribute to the Church. A similar tribute came from Miss Chernoff who said Eileen would make a first-rate musician if she kept at it.

Kathleen felt she was letting the Church down. Something in her rejected music, resisted spending so much energy in so many directions at once—fingering, pedalling, tempo, expression and then, the memorizing. When she practised, her eyes and her arms ached. She got cramps in her fingers. A piece she was learning to play became, with no interval of achievement, a piece she couldn't get through. "Kathleen," Miss Rosen said one day, "are you double jointed?" Another day, she turned and said to Mrs. Lynch, "Has Kathleen ever worn glasses?"

In the Theory classroom, Kathleen felt conspicuous. No matter how far to the back or the side she sat, her Holy Family uniform made her stand out, proclaiming her to be one of many but one who without her many was nothing, a lifeless limb of the Mystical Body. The other children wore what looked like play clothes but might have been school clothes, too. The music school was an extension of their lives, not a departure from everything they knew. Once a boy asked Kathleen what the gold emblem on the pocket of her jumper stood for. Her cheeks flamed as she told him, "Holy Family." The nuns said you were supposed to be proud of your faith, to welcome the chance to talk about it, even to look for chances. Kathleen thought of Saint Peter. "Before the cock crows. . . ."

In Theory II, the trouble she had with the work made her more conspicuous still. Transposing, making up melodies, measuring intervals—it was like arithmetic. Behind the precision of the rules, behind the rigid symbols, there was that same vagueness, something fundamentally potential that it was pointless to try and investigate much less pin down. In class, Kathleen let her mind wander and soon was hopelessly behind. Every so often a question was put to her, always something easy, seldom easy enough. "Kathleen?" Miss Kahn would say, with doubt and apology that were never in her voice when she called Naomi, or Shirley, or Judith, or Aaron, or Nahum, or David. To assume that they knew the lesson was perfectly natural. Their heads were full of notes. Their exercise books were full of music. They enjoyed going to the head of the class and conducting "Hot Cross Buns," or "Robin Goodbye." For a treat, they were taken not to Radio City but to Carnegie Hall where they heard Horowitz, Rubinstein, Josef and Rosina Lhevinne, Jascha Heifetz, Mischa Elman. Music was something they would always have. It was theirs to begin with.

Regularly, the name Eileen Lynch appeared on the monthly recital program. There was always a good crowd down in the auditorium, relatives of every degree, bursting with pride, high standards, high spirits. They stood up to locate friends, waved, called across the rows, visited back and forth, and cast deferential looks towards the seats at the rear where the faculty sat with pencils and pads, ready to make notes on their respective pupils. Sights were to be seen at those recitals, bearded rabbis, or *Chassidim* whose rapt faces spoke of passionate scholarship and of eyestrain. Very old people came, grandparents, granduncles and aunts, all with a love of music and a reverence for the young. That was the wonderful thing about Jewish life, Mrs. Lynch, there by herself, would reflect. There was such a sense of family. (With respect to the monthly recital, Mr. Lynch had put his foot down. "I'd never be able to sit through it," he said.)

Across the aisle from the audience sat the children, all dressed up, their attention divided between each other and the door to the right of the stage. From time to time, this door opened and Miss Ellenbogen looked out to summon a row of students backstage where Mr. Field presided, a casual impresario. If a violinist was on the program, it was Mr. Field who came out from the wings and closed the piano. Applause and cries of "Bravo!" would rise from the audience, and in a gesture that was wholly out of character, he'd bow; then straightening up and brushing the curls back from his forehead, he'd become himself again. Vicki Hana was the official accompanist. She walked onstage a few steps behind the violinist, went around the back of the piano, gave the audience a nod not a bow, and then sat down and waited, beautiful and submissive, for her signal to begin.

A violinist was placed strategically on the program to provoke the greatest possible surprise, pleasure and gratitude from an audience thoroughly familiar with the ritual of the monthly recital. Always, the best beginners led off, followed by an immediate and steady drop in the level of musicianship. But just before the intermission there was always someone very good, to encourage members of the audience whose children had already played to stay for the second half. Then, at the very end of the concert, there'd be a burst of real virtuosity.

Invariably, Eileen Lynch was one of these last few to play. Cool and composed, she walked onstage and over to the piano, curtseyed, sat down, moved the stool back or forward an inch or two, glanced at the pedals, placed her hands in her lap and looked at them, those two trusted colleagues, then raised them to the keyboard, fingers in the curved position. She played Haydn, Clementi, Mozart, Schubert,

Bach—Études, Preludes, Sonatinas, Sonatas. The applause, when she finished, came with a start and went on and on, past praise and into wonder. The Jewish parents were taken with this alien prodigy, so self-controlled and so unassuming. Their congratulations were mixed with curiosity. Mrs. Lynch simply said, "God has been very good to her."

Kathleen's name seldom turned up on the program. The miracle that synchronised the mechanism of memory and muscle, motor and nerve, was usually, in her case, too much to hope for, and even when she was scheduled to play she'd sometimes get excused at the last minute. The plea of a sore throat would often do it. She could also bring on an imitation fever by staying completely under the bedclothes when she woke up in the morning. Once or twice tears had worked.

Less of an ordeal was Miss Rosen's private recital, held in May at her apartment on Riverside Drive. There'd even be a point—standing with her mother outside the door of the apartment—when Kathleen felt as if she were going to a party; then, the door would open and there would be old Mrs. Rosen, who lived with her daughter. She was small and thin and, except for the dark suits she wore, completely unlike Miss Rosen. With a compassionate smile, she led the way to the living room where rows of chairs had been set up, and where Kathleen was at once reminded of her own strangeness, of the crucial something that marked her and forbade any communion with these children she found herself among. Most of them recognized her—as she recognized most of them—but no one spoke to her, or exchanged commiserating looks with her or, after having played, smiles of relief.

One year Miss Rosen announced that she was holding her May recital at Steinway Hall. Kathleen was stricken with regret for the apartment on Riverside Drive. She realized she'd never appreciated it, having to see herself instead on the stage of Horowitz and Rubinstein. She had Steinway Hall and Carnegie Hall confused.

There was a period when children from other parts of the settlement house—the artists, the modern dancers—took to invading the music school, pushing open the black door and plunging down the wide corridor, yelling and laughing. Miss Ellenbogen left her tiny office and dealt with the situation. "If I find you in here again," she said each time, "I'll report you to the Superintendent and you'll be barred from the building." Those episodes caused a rustle of anger among the serious music students and their parents, and the anger was slow to subside. But Kathleen Lynch, momentarily roused, would return at once to one or another of the Marjorie Maynard books, or perhaps a Nancy Drew mystery.

Miss Chernoff had a second piano moved into her room and put her two best pupils, Eileen Lynch and Miriam Kass, on Haydn's Concerto in D Major, scored for two pianos. The friendly competitiveness of the twin keyboards was carried over into the Theory III classroom where, if Miriam wasn't first to raise her hand, Eileen was. Miss Kahn, torn between being fair and giving encouragement, touched her fingers helplessly to the back of her hair, combing the softly curled ends, finally calling, more often than not, on one of the other students, someone less talented but no less eager. The third year textbook had a hard cover with the familiar name, Angela Diller, on the front. *Look over the melodies on pages 11 and 12,* Miss Diller suggested with her characteristic lack of condescension. *Find examples in ¾ meter of the rhythmic designs One-Two-Three and Three-One-Two. . . . Study the following melodies. Notice the form of each: that is, notice the number of phrases; notice which phrases are alike and which are different; notice where the rhythms and melodic shapes are repeated. . . .*

Kathleen became aware of a change in Miss Rosen. The

old exuberance was gone. She sometimes seemed offended. There'd be a pained expression on her face. She'd turn away from the keyboard and look out the window, pressing her full lips together and then releasing them with a sigh. When she spoke, there was something guarded in her voice; her famous patience had clearly become an effort. She gave Kathleen Schumann's "Träumerei," "Because *träumerei* means a kind of dreaming, and I think," she said sadly, "you like to dream." This was a point the nuns were inclined to labor. "Stop woolgathering," they said. "Pay attention." Keep your head where it belongs." "An idle mind is the devil's workshop." The nuns spoke to Mrs. Lynch and told her, "Kathleen is a dreamer. She's always off in the clouds."

Kathleen was left back in Theory II. She got Eileen's "Learning to Listen: the Second Year" intending to use it as a reference and instead she took to copying the completed exercises, changing a beat here, a note there, handing them in as her own work. Week after week, she told the priest, rotating among the four confessionals of Holy Family church, disguising her voice, varying the description of her sin: "I copied." "I cheated." "I borrowed someone else's homework." "I lied." "I stole." "I bore false witness."

Miss Kahn said to Mrs. Lynch, "Kathleen is very sweet," and Kathleen gazed at the floor. Joel and Ari were not sweet, Ruth and Deborah, Shirley and Saul were not sweet. They were sturdy, serious, alert, straightforward and industrious. They were above reproach. Christ had made a mistake.

"Eileen must have an hour's lesson," Miss Chernoff said, and if the Lynches couldn't afford it she'd give the extra half hour free. Mrs. Lynch was overcome and said she thought they could manage the added expense but she'd have to speak to Mr. Lynch. He said, "If she wants to do it for nothing why not let her?" But Mrs. Lynch thought that would cast some reflection on the Church.

In Theory IV, Angela Diller raised questions that seemed to concern the soul as well as the mechanics of music. *What is a fundamental? What is an overtone? What is sympathetic vibration? What is tonal magnetism?* Eileen took it all in her stride. She accepted music. The subleties of its language were no obstacle to her, the complexity of its doctrine no drawback. She finished Theory and went on into Counterpoint.

With luck, her mother's prayers, and two years' exposure to the work, Kathleen got out of Theory II and into Theory III where she tried to "look over," to "examine," to "notice" and ended up failing to understand the complicated hierarchy by which the notes of the scale were governed. There were dominants and subdominants, mediants and submediants, tonics and supertonics, augmented fourths, diminished fifths. Turning the pages of the hard-covered text, Kathleen knew that no effort of hers would ever bring harmony to those divergent factions.

Eileen played Debussy, limpid pieces with names like the titles of fairy tales—"The Little Shepherd," "The Minstrels," "The Girl with the Flaxen Hair." She sat at the piano tilted slightly back and to the right, the better to send her strength into her long, narrow, blunt-tipped fingers that could take tenths with ease. At this stage, Kathleen was usually stretched out on the living room sofa with the complete works of Jane Austen, a single volume. Music—someone else's music—had become for her a place where she could hide and concentrate. Eileen's playing made it all the easier for her to lose herself in that crowd of spirited girls, elegible bachelors, governesses, spinsters, scoundrels, vicars and officers who went for walks, attended balls, played the pianoforte, sang, drew, fell (unhappily) in love and were married (happily).

For the Steinway Hall recital, Kathleen was to play "Träumerei" and the "Moment Musical #3" by Schubert.

"Think of a single moment," Miss Rosen said wearily, "a moment set apart, devoted to music. Each second must dance." Kathleen saw black seconds, swarming like insects. She began to neglect "Moment Musical" in favor of "Träumerei." Though it was Schumann who was said to be so difficult, she could play it through without mistakes, and it was short enough for her to pay attention to feeling and expression. She found she could even enjoy her own rendition of the piece. She thought of Carnegie Hall, of Horowitz and Rubinstein. She might not disgrace their stage.

But the room in Steinway Hall had no stage. It was a small room with a high ceiling and two big windows, partly open on that warm May afternoon, letting in sounds of the cross-town traffic on Fifty-seventh Street. There were blue velvet curtains at the windows, and a blue carpet ran the length of the aisle separating two sections of gilt chairs. At first Kathleen was confused; then she was oddly disappointed at finding herself in a different place from the one she was prepared for, a place less intimidating but so much less grand.

Miss Rosen, handing out programs at the door, said to Mrs. Lynch, as though they rarely met, "How nice to see you."

"On such a lovely occasion," Mrs. Lynch replied. The room was already crowded, and she had to take a place at the back but she found a good spot, in the middle of a row with a fine view of the keyboard—though she'd only just settled herself when a white-bearded rabbi came down the aisle and indicated the two chairs on either side of her.

"May I trouble you to tell me if these are taken?" he asked.

Mrs. Lynch said they weren't, and the rabbi gestured towards the back of the room. An old woman, a younger woman and a man came down the aisle. "Here," Mrs. Lynch said, "I'll move in so you can all sit together."

The rabbi bowed. "You're very kind," he said.

At five past three, Miss Rosen went forward and closed the windows; then, she stepped over to the head of the aisle, clasped her hands low in front of her, smiled and said, "I want to welcome you to our annual recital. We've all worked very hard and we think we have a very fine program. Now, let's relax and enjoy ourselves." She took a seat in the empty front row on the audience side. Across the way, Judith Bernstein left the aisle seat and opened the program with "Sleep, Baby, Sleep" and "Raindrops." The applause, when she finished, was generous, an outburst of good will brought under control only when Joel Kauffman went forward to play "Song of the Boatman" and "Bergerette." The applause for him was less generous, as though the audience had suddenly been reminded of the length of the program and the reserves of patience needed to see it through. Sandra Tabor, who was next with "Air" by Henry Purcell and Haydn's "Theme in G Major," got an even more measured reception, under cover of which the rabbi turned to Mrs. Lynch. "My grandson," he said, pointing to the fifth name on the program, Ari Davidson. Mrs. Lynch showed him Kathleen's name. "Lynch," the rabbi said, stroking his patriarchal beard. "I think I've heard her play."

"You may be thinking of my older girl," Mrs. Lynch said. "She studies with Miss Chernoff." The rabbi told this to his daughter-in-law.

Marsha Stein played "Gavotte and Musette," and when she'd finished, someone in the back of the room took a fit of coughing that was still going on when Ari Davidson seated himself at the piano. The rabbi's grandson waited with perfect composure for the disturbance to die down and with the same perfect composure he played his two numbers. Mrs. Lynch turned to the rabbi and whispered, "Excellent! *Ex*cellent!"

These two pieces, like everything else on the program so far, were ones Kathleen had studied, though now if someone had asked her to play them or any of the others she'd have had to begin as painfully as if she'd never seen the notes before. Music went right through her. She learned it and forgot it. After today she'd forget the "Moment Musical." She'd even forget "Träumerei," the only piece she'd ever learned that seemed to come naturally.

David Lewis was sent back to his place with a spurt of applause that stopped well before Ruth Marcus left the chair beside Kathleen's. It was impossible to ignore that empty chair but it was possible to get used to it and to find comfort in the fact that it was still someone else's turn, though this was false comfort. Ruth Marcus returned. Blindly, Kathleen made her way out into the aisle, up to the front of the room and over to the piano, where she turned to the audience—faces and figures massed together, all with one demand: Play. She made her curtsey and meekly sat down and faced the keys, the black and the white like sets of identical doors, some of them sham, some that would yield and open. She placed her hands in position and started off on the "Moment Musical." "Make each second dance," Miss Rosen had said, but Kathleen's fingers were cold and stiff. They dragged through the statement and restatement and the final hammering home of the theme. There was a crack of applause, a punishment which Kathleen accepted. But relief had begun to thaw her frozen fingers—she was halfway through. Now there was only "Träumerei." She looked at the keyboard. " '*Träumerei*' means a kind of dreaming," Miss Rosen had said, "and I think you like to dream." The nuns said, "Come down to earth." "Keep your mind where it belongs." "Stop dreaming." Kathleen raised her hands to the keys. Dreams were her sin and her salvation, her fall and redemption. She offered them now, note by note.

The rabbi turned to Mrs. Lynch. "Dear lady," he said, "your child is a musician."

Printed in the USA
CPSIA information can be obtained
at www.ICGtesting.com
JSHW022003270524
63872JS00004B/59

9 781531 507350